Kane & Cowboy: Ou 2

By Mel Pate

Copyright page

Chapter 1

Kane

My chest feels warm seeing Mia smiling. She deserves all the happiness in the world after what she's been through. Growing up in an abusive home and raising herself took a toll. Now, she needs someone to take care of her. Show her how a real man loves and cares for a woman. I'm going to be that man now that she's legal. I'm done waiting to see what will happen between her and Cowboy.

Giving her space to see what she wants has been killing me. Mia knows we're both attracted to her, but I've been putting her before me and my wants, even though it guts me. I've waited long enough, and I'm making my move. The time we've spent together over the past month proves what I already knew. She's mine.

This birthday party with everyone around who cares about her is just what she needs. I let my eyes roam over her while she laces her new riding boots.

Her long, wavy dark hair cascades over her shoulders to the ground while she's bent over. I look lower to the hint of cleavage peeking above her top. Down to the tight as fuck jeans that are hugging her full round ass and thick thighs. The kind of curves you can hang onto and know they'll handle a good hard fuck. Damn, my dick is at half-mass and rising fast. This isn't the time or place to be getting hard.

I step close after she finishes lacing her boots and stands. If anyone is giving her riding lessons, it'll be me. Cowboy sees what I'm doing and goes to her other side, and we both walk with her to her new motorcycle.

I side-eye Cowboy, wondering what he's doing. Hell, he pushes her away at every turn, even though we can all see he wants her. Didn't she tell him she was tired of his head games?

Mia grabs the handlebars and throws her leg over to straddle it, and I place my hands on her back to steady her. Then I shoot Cowboy my fuck off look. He gives me one right back, stepping closer to her other side, making me grit my teeth.

I have always considered him my brother, both in the military and now in the MC. But I won't let him, or anyone, screw this up with Mia. She will be mine, and I'll claim her as soon as she accepts me.

Mia turns to me with her sparkling smile, and I return it. She tilts her head to the side, studying my face, and her eyebrows draw together. Can she sense the tension I'm feeling?

She turns, looking at Cowboy, and her shoulders stiffen. Her smile falters, replaced by a confused look. "What now?" she says with a sigh.

"We're going to get you started with your first lesson," Cowboy says, and his eyes flicker up to me before settling back on Mia. Well, shit, the last thing she needs is us fighting. I grit my teeth and keep my mouth shut for now.

"Fine, but be nice," she says, giving him a pointed look, and Cowboy nods.

I started by going over where everything was: clutch, brakes, turn signals, and how to shift. Once I finished, Cowboy went over how to start it and ease the clutch out.

"Stay in first gear, and we'll jog alongside you until you get the hang of it," I tell her. Mia pulls in the clutch and starts the engine. I keep my hands on her while she eases it out and takes off.

Damn, her smile is as bright as the sun as Cowboy, and I stay next to her on the first pass around the parking lot. It doesn't take long before she rides big circles and cuts her lines like a pro.

Everyone in the club's at the edge of the lot, watching. Everything's going great until a damn prospect comes over to have some fun.

I know what he's up to before he opens his mouth when he saddles up next to Cowboy. "You seem a little tense, man. Why don't you go take a seat and let me give her a few lessons," he says, and I don't miss the insinuation. He doesn't mean anything by it. Hell, we all know Cowboy has been fighting his feelings for Mia, but poking a bear is a dangerous thing.

Cowboy turns and squares up on him, taking him by the throat. "What the fuck did you say? Cowboy's boiling with rage and is ready to rip his head off.

The prospect raises his hands in surrender and speaks through Cowboy's death grip. " I'm just having a little fun."

I grab Cowboy, pulling him off the poor kid. "He's just riling you up. Calm down," I say, staring him in the eye. Shit, he's the fucking VP. He needs to control himself better. Cowboy has always been the calculated one. But when it comes to Mia, he loses his shit fast.

His face is red with anger as he shoves me off him. "Get off me, Kane," Cowboy says, and I shake my head.

When I turn, I see Mia riding towards the gate and the guard opening it at her approach.

Fuck, what's she doing? Bo comes jogging over to us with an angry face. "You're both fucking idiots!" he yells, running past us and jumping on his bike.

Rage boils inside me as Blaze and Gia prevent me from moving by blocking my path.

"You two," she spits, pointing at us. Blaze takes her by the waist and tells her to stay out of it, but she's not listening.

"Stop your shit before you hurt her more," she says, and I freeze. I wouldn't do anything to hurt Mia—my chest tightens at the thought.

"Stop your fighting and ask yourselves what Mia wants. Or better yet, did it cross your mind to ask her?" she growls, looking between us.

Shit, no, I've been taking things slow. I was staying in the flirty friend zone until her birthday. I look at Cowboy, who is staring at me. So many emotions flash in his eyes.

"You need to back off and let me make her happy," I say in a low, dangerous tone.

Cowboy's eyes narrow on me, and his jaw ticks. "I'm not going anywhere."

Gia leans forward, even angrier than before. "See, this is what I'm talking about. Stop! Talk to her, actually talk, and stop fighting."

I look down at Gia and study her face. She knows something we don't. I give her a firm nod in understanding, then look at Cowboy. "When Bo brings her back, we all talk. It's time we listen to her."

Cowboy looks like he's in deep thought, then gives me a chin lift before going to the bar for a drink.

I'm rooted to my spot. The thought of her riding with no experience has my stomach in knots. Especially if she's upset while riding. My eyes focus on the gate until I see her and Bo coming down the road.

I take a deep breath and relax my hands. I didn't realize I had them fisted so tight. My fingers are stiff, and my palms have indentations from pressure.

Relief floods me when they ride through the gate and park in front of the clubhouse. I take long strides in her direction. I need to see she's OK. If anything happens to her, I don't know what I'll do.

Bo looks over his shoulder and notices me approaching them. Then his gaze goes past me. I look, and Cowboy is coming up behind me. Bo makes my steps falter when he shakes his head no to both of us.

I halt in my spot, and Cowboy stops next to me. Shit, does Mia not want to speak to us? "No more arguing," I say, knowing Cowboy hears me. He also hears the finality of my words.

"We ask her what she wants," he says, crossing his arms over his chest as Mia enters the clubhouse and Bo walks to us.

"You may think this is none of my business, but I'm making it mine. Mia is like a sister to me. Has been for years. You need to talk. Actually, ask her what she wants. This back-and-forth shit you're doing is hurting her," Bo says, looking between us.

Anyone else trying to stick their nose in between me and my woman, I would beat their ass. But there's something different about Bo. The way he looks at us, I can tell he doesn't just want to protect her. He wants things to work out.

"Thanks, man," I say, slapping him on the shoulder. He gives me a chin lift before walking away.

Cowboy looks concerned when I turn to him. "Are you ready to go talk? Hear what she has to say with no attitude?" I ask, keeping my voice even.

"Ya, I'm just worried she's going to tell me to go fuck myself," he says, and I chuckle.

We walk up the steps to the clubhouse together, and I side-eye him. "Would you blame her after the way you've acted?" I can't hide my grin.

"No, but I can't walk away," he sighs. I feel his words down to my bones. Shit, I feel the same way. I'm not the one who has been going from showing interest to treating her like crap. That's all on him.

Chapter 2

Mia

I lace my boots up as fast as possible, which is hard, with my fingers shaking with excitement. Although I have my license, thanks to Bo and Gia, I've never had a vehicle of my own. I can't believe they got me a motorcycle. Now, I won't have to ride with Gia; I can ride beside her.

My cheeks ache from smiling so hard as I stand and walk to my new bike. It's Royal Blue, my favorite color, and it sits low enough for my short legs to reach the ground. Being 5 foot 6 can be a pain sometimes.

As I get on, I feel Kane's large hands holding my back. The warmth from his palms soaks into my skin, causing tingles to erupt. They spread through me like they do every time he touches me. The man is gorgeous but confusing. I turn my head and smile at him for helping me. He has stayed close since the last time my padre attacked me.

I look into his warm, dark eyes, and my insides melt. Kane is 6 feet 2 and a wet dream. His long dark hair goes just past his shoulders, a strong sculpted face with a thick goatee, muscles for days, and his ass. Nope, I won't think about how amazing it looks in those jeans.

Examining his face closer, I see something's off. Then I feel a presence at my side, and I turn. Cowboy's next to me. His eyes are soft, hungry-looking even. He's mouthwatering but confusing. One minute, he's protective and flirty and has my body craving his touch. The next minute, he's an asshole pushing me away.

I can't trust he won't flip and be an ass to me in five seconds. When I question him, he says he's going to help. Hmmm. "Be nice," I say, and he nods. Hopefully, he keeps his word.

I try to relax and listen carefully as they go over everything. Most of this I already knew. I may be 18, but I have raised myself, gone to school, and trained six days a week at the gym. Not to mention, I graduated high school with a 4.0 GPA at 17.

Everything is going great as I cruise around the parking lot. Until I look up ahead, seeing them fighting again. Kane has a hold on Cowboy, and they look like they'll kill each other. I'm so over this. One day, just. One day, I wanted to enjoy myself with no drama—none of their bullshit.

I lean, turning the bike towards the gate, and angry tears fill my eyes. The prospect on guard duty sees me coming and opens it as I approach. I hear Bo yelling my name, but I don't stop.

I just need a few minutes. What's wrong with me? Why am I attracted to two men? One that holds back, showing me he doesn't feel the same, and one is an asshole. It's more than attraction, and I know it. Over the past month spending time with Kane and our late-night talks, I know I'm in love with him. But I can't just make my feelings for Cowboy disappear. I've tried, and when Cowboy is close, Kane backs off. Who does that if they're interested in you? Maybe I need to get away from both of them now that I'm 18.

I hear a motorcycle coming up behind me, and I hope it's Bo or Gia because I don't want to see Cowboy or Kane until I clear my head. I see the old gas station up ahead and pull in, shutting my bike off. I wipe the tears off my cheeks before I turn my head, seeing Bo.

He shuts his bike off and drops the kickstand. When his eyes meet mine, I see the worry in them. "Are you ok?" he asks.

"Ya, I just needed to think," I say, trying to keep more tears from falling.

Bo dismounts and wraps his arms around me, pulling me into his chest. I melt into him and squeeze him tight. His hugs are always the best, and I know I never have to hide how I feel with him.

"You need to talk to them," Bo says, and I tilt my head, looking up at his face.

"Bo, I love two men who should be brothers, but fight when they're with me."

"Have you told them how you feel? What you want?" he asks me with an eyebrow raised.

"No, but we need to talk. I'm so angry at them," I say, frustrated, kicking a rock across the parking lot.

"Come on, let's get back so the others don't worry," Bo says, kissing my head.

When we ride through the gates, I notice out of my peripheral vision everyone looking at us. I ride to the front of the clubhouse, park, and go straight inside. I want to wash my face and compose myself before I talk to them.

When I enter the main room, I see Hunter cradling a towel to his chest, talking to it, and the towel moves. My curiosity gets the best of me, and I stop at his side on my way to the stairs. Looking down at his arms, I see a black kitten curled up. It's so cute.

"Where did you find it?" I ask, reaching my hand out and stroking the top of its head.

"I was out back earlier and kept hearing a meow next to the porch. She was hungry, so I gave her some milk, and then she snuggled right up to me," Hunter says with a grin.

I hear a noise and see The Man swoop down and land on Hunter's shoulder. He's getting braver with people, especially the guys who constantly feed him nuts and play with him.

"What's that?" The Man asks, staring at the cat. He speaks so clearly for a parrot.

"This is a pussy cat," Hunter says, and I shake my head. I know better than anyone to be careful what you say to him. He repeats everything.

"Pussy, pussy," the man says, and I cover my mouth to stifle a laugh. I knew that would happen; I just knew it.

The cat seems annoyed and jumps out of Hunter's arms and walks around the room. I stand next to Hunter's wheelchair and smile as we watch it explore for a few minutes. When it gets curious about The Man's six-foot cage, I start to intervene and get her, but Hunter takes my wrist. "She's just looking around," he says.

I watch for a few minutes until she walks below The Man's perch, where the litter box is. My eyes go to the Man to see if he's noticed her in his enormous cage. It doesn't take long until he screeches, taking off.

I look back into the cage, and there is the cat hunkered down, doing its business in his litter box. The Man swoops into the cage screeching, "Bad Pussy, Bad Pussy!" The cat lunges out of the litter box and, at full speed, flies across the room onto a table, knocking over a pitcher of beer and plastic cups. I gasp at the sight.

Prospects are yelling. Some are laughing as I watch in horror. The man is determined to chase the cat down, yelling, "Bad Pussy!" Outcasts are chasing after them. Furniture is being turned and drinks are getting spilled everywhere. The poor cat is skidding across the slick wood floors, trying to stop, but hits the wall. As soon as it gets its bearings again, it takes off, heading for us at top speed.

It's running to Hunter. He leans forward in his wheelchair with his arms opened wide to catch it.

The cat jumps, and everything seems to move in slow motion when I see its razor-sharp claws out in mid-air. It lands on Hunter's chest and digs in deep. Hunter throws his head back, yelling. "Oh fuck!"

"When's the last time a pussy made you yell that?" A prospect yells. The room burst into laughter.

"Someone, tell me they caught all that on video. Please, we could make a fortune." Someone else says.

The room is a disaster, and Gia is placing the man on his perch. "Time out for you, buddy," she tells him.

My eyes widen as I take in the destruction here, while everyone around me laughs or comments.

"No one is putting anything on the internet," Hunter says as he pulls the cat's claws from his chest.

It's like complete chaos around me. My eyes meet Gia's, and it hits us at the same time. I cover my mouth with my hands as she cups her face, and we laugh.

I know one thing: I'm not cleaning this mess up. I glance around, then back at her. We both shake our heads and go upstairs.

Once in my room, I shut the door and breathed a sigh. Walking to the end of my bed, I sit and drop my head into my hands. I need to tell Kane and Cowboy everything. Not just my feelings, but how their behavior has made me feel, and I need space. I need to move on from them.

A loud knock on the door pulls me from my thoughts, and I raise my head. "Come in," I yell.

The door opens, and Cowboy steps in. His dark hair and eyes are captivating. He may think that Cowboy hat he wears hides them, but they don't. My eyes travel lower to his bare chest and ripped abs, only partially covered by his leather cut. The man never wears shirts; I bite my lip and force my eyes back up before I get aroused. He knows what he does to me; he has to.

Kane stops standing next to Cowboy and shit. Having them both here, in my bedroom, has my mouth going dry. I need to compose myself.

"Please close the door so we can talk," I say, standing. It's time I speak my mind. I've been quiet long enough. Cowboy gets a worried expression, but closes the door when he turns back to me. Stepping forward, I gaze into his eyes.

"You're a Yoyo. One minute you're nice; the next, an asshole. I go from thinking you feel the same for me as I do you, to you jumping people for speaking to me or treating me like crap. It stops now. Tell me what your problem is. Just spit it out." I need honest answers.

Cowboy's face looks pained, and he removes his hat, shoving his hair and gripping it. "I'm crazy about you, Mia, but you're too good for me, and I'm too old for you," he says, frustrated.

So, this is about age and what he thinks of himself. "How old are you, Cowboy?"

"28," he says, then flexes his jaw.

"And you?" I point at Kane.

"27," he answers, and I nod before looking back at Cowboy.

"Let me get this right," I say, pointing at him. "You've been an ass for a month because you have problems with YOUR age and what you think of YOURSELF, and you've been projecting it onto me?"

Cowboy freezes, and his face contorts in confusion. Ya, he looks confused.

I turn to Kane, who is watching us closely. "I won't come between the two of you. That patch makes you brothers, friends, hell, your family, as far as the Outcasts are concerned. No matter how I feel about you, things can't continue like they are."

Kane starts to speak, but I hold my hand up. "It's time for me to talk. We met at the worst of times after I was attacked. You both took care of me. You made me feel safe, and the chemistry was off the charts. But Kane, you backed away and left as soon as Cowboy showed interest. A man doesn't do that if he cares." I shake my head. I've been fooling myself this whole time.

Kane steps close so we are almost touching and takes my hand. "Slow down, Mia. Tell us, tell me what you want." His eyes search mine. They're so warm and caring I could get lost in them.

"I've wanted you both from the beginning. It's never been a competition. I wanted you both equally. At first, it was physical attraction, but that grew into much more. It's like you are two sides to the same coin," I say, looking between them. I only hope they can understand.

"But that isn't possible; your actions have proven that. I'm falling in love with you both, and I have to stop it now before we all get hurt." I look at Cowboy, and he looks so remorseful. But I've seen how he is.

"Cowboy, you can't stand someone even speaking to me, more or less touching me. Add to that the other issues you have going on with our age difference. We need to stay away from each other." It's painful to say, but I have to.

I look back at Kane and pull my hand out of his. "I think of you as more than a friend, Kane. The time we've spent together has made me fall for you." I shake my head and back away from them. "But I need to distance myself now. Every time Cowboy is near, you pull away. That tells me you don't feel the same for me. What man will move aside so another can move in? Not one who cares or," I stop myself before I say loves. "Anyway, you wouldn't step aside if you cared. I deserve better than that. Someone who's all in." My eyes fill with tears as I get the words out.

I walk around them and open the door. "You need to leave."

"Mia," Kane's voice is pained, but I shake my head and stare into the hallway, waiting for them to leave.

Once they are out the door, I close it and twist the lock. My heart feels like it's being ripped out of my chest, and my vision blurs from the tears. Once I reach the bed, I kick my shoes off, remove my pants, and jerk the covers back.

All I want is a good hard cry and sleep. Gia was wrong when she told me about polyamorous relationships and how a lot of couples build lives with families. It won't work with them. I bury my face in the pillow and let it all out. This is the last time I will allow myself to shed a tear over them, I promise myself. If I have to move into an apartment when they're finished for some distance, then I will.

Chapter 3

Cowboy

I shut the door to Mia's room and turned to Kane. "What the hell just happened in there?" I yell out to him and myself. I can't walk away.

"Fuck, we both screwed up," Kane says, and his face shows the same pain I feel. "I don't have a problem sharing. You're my brother. Shit, we're family. I thought by giving her space, I was giving her what she wanted, even though it was killing me."

My mouth drops open at his words. I've never considered sharing a woman before. I'm a possessive man.

Kane doesn't miss my shock, steps close and talks low. "Tell me the image of her plump lips around your cock while I slide mine into her warm wet pussy doesn't get you hard?"

A vision of that scenario flashes in my mind, making my dick twitch. Shit, that's hot as hell, and a groan escapes me.

Kane grins and nods. "I've never shared a woman in my life but Mia," Kane says, pointing to the door. "She is everything to me. Mine. But the thought of us sharing her, claiming her, and building a family makes me hard as fuck. She could be ours if you can get past your shit."

I look at her door and feel my chest tighten. There's no walking away; I'm in love with her. I look back at Kane; I really look at him. We're already family. Us claiming Mia and building a future with children is what I want.

"You're right. She's ours, and it's time we claimed her," I say with finality.

I see movement past Kane and look. Gia is walking toward us. I stand straighter as she approaches. "If you two are out here and she's in there, I assume you still haven't pulled your head out of your asses." She looks between us, and I groan in frustration.

"Did she tell you what she wanted?" she asks.

"Yes," is all I say.

"Then, if you're just standing here, you're not half as smart as I thought you were. Either walk away or make her happy and never let her go. These are the two options. It's not difficult." Gia stares at me with a raised brow.

"Neither of us can let her go," I growl.

11

"Good," Gia says with a cocky look, before walking away.

I turn to Kane, and his face is firm. "How are we going to handle this? She's pissed and hurt?" he asks.

"We go in there and tell her how things will be. We don't leave even if she tells us to. We both want to claim her as ours, and that's what we'll do when she's ready. We may have to prove it to her," I say, pointing to her door.

"We convince her to give us a shot, that we're not going anywhere. We trust each other. Now we have to convince her to trust us," Kane says, and I nod in agreement, going over in my mind what this will mean.

"We have no secrets; we share everything. That includes kids, not just her as our woman and wife. Can you commit to that?" I ask Kane.

"Hell yes." His words hold finality as he steps closer. "She won't believe us at first. She'll fight us, push us away. But we can't let that happen—Mia's right. I should have fought for and stood beside her, and I didn't," Kane says with a remorseful look.

"I shouldn't have been an ass and treated her like I did. She's smart, beautiful and funny. Fuck, I'm in love with her. There's no one else for me," I admit.

Kane's eyes tell me he feels the same way. "Then we have to prove to her that we're all in. No letting her run." His expression is stern and I feel resolve wash over me. Mia doesn't realize how much her life will change with both of us claiming her.

"Cowboy," Kane says in a gravelly voice, getting my attention. "If you act like a dick again, you'll have me to deal with."

I hear the threat in his tone. Many underestimate him because of his SOCM training, not me. He's trained and battle-tested like the rest of us.

I nod and step closer, squaring up to him, knowing that we are evenly matched. "It's not going to happen. But Kane, if you hurt her by pulling away again, you'll deal with me," I growl. He smirks at me and nods in understanding.

I reach out, grasping the doorknob, but it won't budge. "She locked it," I say, looking at Kane.

He grins and then says he'll be right back. A few minutes later, he returns with a small black case. When he unzips it, I smile, seeing the tools inside. Kane has the locked picked-in minutes.

While he puts the tools away, I ease the door open, seeing Mia's form under the covers in the center of the bed. All that's visible is her long, dark hair splayed over the pillows. The covers are pulled up, covering her face, and she's in the fetal position.

I open the door wider before walking to stand next to the bed and looking down at her. Mia is everything I've ever wanted. I remove my cut, lay it on the nightstand, and then begin undressing, leaving only my boxers on.

Kane's doing the same on the other side of the bed. We both raise the covers and climb in. I curl up beside her and groan when I feel her soft, warm body touching mine. She's not wearing pants. Please let her be wearing underwear, or I don't know if I can control myself. I slide my arm around her upper body, snuggling close behind her, and press my now-rising shaft into her lush ass. Damn, everything about this feels right.

Kane gets in bed, saddling up to her other side, wrapping his arm around her waist, and burying his nose in her hair. When he inhales deeply, a low rumble sounds from his chest. I know right then we're both fucked.

Mia stirs, and a whimper escapes from under the covers before she pulls them down, revealing her face. Once her sleepy eyes focus, she looks at Kane and then at me with furrowed brows. "What are you two doing in here?"

"You're ours, and we're yours. We're not leaving, no matter what you say." I tighten my hold on her.

Mia struggles, turning to her back with both of us holding her, and I allow it. It will only make it easier to pin her down so we can explain things to her.

"You said your peace earlier; now it's our turn," Kane says, and she jerks her head in his direction.

"You need to leave. I said all I have to say." The pain I see in her eyes makes my chest tighten. When she pushes the covers down and starts to raise, I know what we need to do.

I throw my leg over hers closest to me, firmly pinning it in place. Then I take her hand and raise it above her head. Kane follows my lead, doing the same on his side. We have her pinned now, and she can't move.

"Yes, you said plenty earlier. Now it's our turn," Kane says, gently kissing her forehead to calm her. Her face looks worried, and the last thing I want with her past.

"You're right. I was an ass. But that's over now. You're mine, ours," I say, glancing over at Kane. Mia needs to know we're both all in. Mia searches my face to see if I mean what I'm saying. Her expression softens, and she looks doubtful, her eyes well with tears.

"You were right about me too," Kane says, and she looks at him with the same doubts she showed me. "I thought I was putting your wants and needs above mine by giving you space to figure out what you wanted. But fuck that, you're mine." Kane leans in close and meets her gaze. The hunger showing in his eyes is the same as I feel.

Mia shakes her head in disbelief.

"We'll prove it every day. We're not going anywhere, Mia. Not tonight, not tomorrow, ever. We'll give you some time, but this is happening," I say firmly. Her body relaxes under mine, and I loosen my hold.

Mia's big brown eyes stare into mine, and her lips part. "How do I know you won't change your mind or start fighting again?" she asks.

"Because we talked and worked everything out," I say. She shifts herself, getting more comfortable, and her hip brushes my dick. Fuck, the simple touch has me a full mast and aching. The feel of her soft, curvy body against mine and under my leg is driving me crazy.

"Worked what out?" Her expression is confused, looking from me to Kane.

"Mia, the thought of sharing you isn't a problem. It's a turn-on. You're ours. I want a life with you, hell, a family. When you're ready, we'll claim you," Kane says, studying her face.

I can tell she still doesn't believe us, and so can Kane. Without warning, Kane growls, leaning down and taking those full, juicy lips with his.

Mia jolts in surprise, then relaxes as Kane's mouth moves over hers. At first, she doesn't respond to him, then she returns it. It's the most erotic thing I've ever witnessed, and I press myself into her. Releasing the hand above her head, I slowly trail it down her arm and over her collarbone.

When I run my fingertips down between her breasts, lowering the sheet more as I go, she moans into Kane's mouth and pulls back, panting. Mia's face is flushed, and I can see her nipples are hard, even through her shirt and bra. I push myself further into her hip for some much-needed relief as she brings her fingers to her lips, touching them as if remembering the feeling of Kane's kiss.

I can't stand it anymore and cup her face, bringing it close to mine. She lowers her fingers and stares into my eyes. "Mine," I say as I close my eyes and taste heaven when our lips touch.

Molding our lips together, I explore them slowly. Then, running the tip of my tongue over the crease of her mouth, I coach her to open for me. When she does, I delve deep to explore. My tongue massaged hers, making us both groan out loud.

Mia runs her hand up around my neck and pulls me close. Hell, yes, I think, tilting my head to the side for a better angle and gripping a handful of her hair.

She squirms beneath me, and I hear Kane's voice. "Do you need us to help you out, dreamcatcher?"

I feel Kane's hand brush up against my leg as he traces her body beneath us. Fuck, Mia writhes under me. Whatever he's doing has her aroused. I pull back from the kiss and look down at her.

Red rosy cheeks, eyes dilated, and chest heaving. "Are you wet, baby?" I ask, but I already know the answer.

Mia bites her bottom lip and nods. Shit, she's beautiful like this. I release her hair and run my hand down her neck and over her large breast, cupping it. Gently flexing my hand to massage it. "Say the word, baby, and we'll make you see stars."

Mia looks hesitant, and I freeze, as does Kane.

"What is it, Mia?" Kane says, leaning higher on his elbow and cupping her face with one hand. "You can tell us anything."

Mia nods and takes a deep breath. "I need to know that you meant what you both said. That I'm truly what you want and we'll be a family. So, we need to wait before we go further," she says, and my chest clenches. We're going to have to prove ourselves after being dicks.

"We'll wait as long as you need Mia," Kane says, kissing her forehead.

When he pulls back, I take her chin and make her look at me. "We're not going anywhere. We'll prove it, Mia, whatever it takes," I say, and she nods. But I see her thinking. There's something she's not saying.

"What else, baby? Talk to us," I encourage her. I want nothing holding us back.

Mia bites on the inside of her cheek, looking between us, but I see her steel herself. "I'm not naïve enough to think you two haven't been with other women. I want you to get tested before we do anything." Her eyes look concerned at what our response will be, and her cheeks flush.

I look at Kane and he nods at me. I look back at Mia. "Baby, I will go tomorrow and get it done. Don't be embarrassed about wanting to protect yourself. Hell, I would be upset if you didn't. But just so you know, I've never touched a woman without a raincoat. And I wouldn't do anything to put you in danger," I say, and relief washes over her face.

She turns, looking at Kane, waiting for his reply. "I'll get tested too. I never went without a rubber before. But Mia, understand something," he says, leaning down close so they are almost touching. "There will never be anything between us," he growls out and grinds himself into her, making a whimper escape her lips.

Fucking hell, I'm hard and throbbing. I rub against her for some relief and dip my head, biting her earlobe. "Get some sleep, baby," I growl low in her ear. We all need rest after today, and I need to sleep with her in my arms.

Chapter 4

Mia

I wake up feeling hot and try to move but can't. When I open my eyes, I realize I'm lying on a hard chest. Last night come flooding back. Kane and Cowboy came into my room while I was asleep and listening to their promises. I squeeze my eyes closed and take a breath through my nose. Warm cedar and pine, maybe? The scent is intoxicating. Can I trust them? The last thing I want are things returning to the way they were.

Damn, I've never slept so well, though. I've been out of my padre's house for over a month now. But after all the years of being hit and dragged out of my bed in the middle of the night, it's hard to get over. I still have nightmares occasionally. Although, the late-night talks with Kane have helped some. Only time will tell if they're telling the truth.

Shit, I have to meet Sal and the construction crew at Big C's old gym this morning. According to Gia, Iron Maiden will open it after it's renovated. As quickly and quietly as I can, I rise off of Kane's chest and remove Cowboy's arm from around my waist. Crawling to the bottom of the bed, I grab clothes from the dresser before going into the bathroom to get ready.

Oh shit, I whisper when I see my reflection in the mirror. I forgot to braid my hair before bed so it wouldn't get tangled. It's too freaking long, almost to my waist now. Maybe I should get it cut.

I quickly dress, brush my teeth and hair, and grab my birth control pills, taking one. As I scoop a handful of water from under the tap so I can swallow it, I wonder if one day I can stop taking them. I only started them to help regulate my periods. They seem to have helped with cramping, too. No time to think about it now.

Easing the bathroom door open, I see the guys are still fast asleep. Cowboy's snoring makes me grin. I glance at Kane's chiseled face; he looks like a Greek god curled up with a pillow. I grab my boots and put them on before exiting the room with my files and legal pad. A fast breakfast and coffee are what I need—definitely lots of coffee.

Jogging down the stairs, I reach the main room and see it's neat again. I pause mid-stride in shock, looking around. Gia or Blaze must have made the guys clean it up. Walking past the man's cage, I grin, seeing him on his perch and the cat on a small bed in the corner. They made peace with each other; I guess. "Morning Man," I say as I pass by.

"Morning, Morning," he replies. The cat barely lifts its head before going back to its nap.

I enter the dining room and lay my things down to grab coffee and food. Several prospects and Hunter are already eating. "Morning," I say to everyone as I make my way to the breakfast bar.

"Morning," they murmur. I'm glad I'm not the only one who's not a morning person around here.

I eat quickly and drink my coffee. Just as I finish, Gia comes in and gets her food, sitting beside me and leaning close. "Are you ok?"

I look at her and can't hide my smile. "Ya, I'm good."

Gia looks at me closely before returning my smile. "You're meeting with the crew this morning at the gym, right?"

I swallow the food in my mouth and nod. "Ya, you said you needed the gym ready as fast as possible."

Gia takes a drink of coffee and leans in close. "Iron Maiden is retiring from MMA and wants to open a gym and offer defense classes. She hasn't officially announced her retirement yet, though. So, keep it quiet." I'm sure she can see the shock on my face.

Iron Maiden inspires all women and what we can become. A lot of her fans will be disappointed, but I'm happy she's coming here to Freedom. I give Gia a nod in understanding. I'll be quiet about who will lease it and what's going in once it opens until its public knowledge.

After I take my dishes into the kitchen and rinse them, I grab my files and legal pad, ready to head out. I stop, looking around the dining room. "Who's up for taking me to meet Sal?" I hate having to depend on them, but it won't be for long since I have a bike now. I need to get good enough to get my motorcycle endorsement.

"I will," Hunter says, rolling back from the table. "I need some fresh air, anyway. Besides, I'd like to see what changes you're doing to the old gym."

I smile at him as I approach his side. "Thanks, Hunter; I know it's a pain driving me around, but it won't be for long."

"Don't worry about it. Gives me a reason to get out of here," he says as we leave the clubhouse. I jog down the steps as he rolls down the ramp to the van.

Once we arrive at Pop's old gym, Hunter turns the engine off as I gather my things in my arms.

"I can't believe Pop's didn't want to move the business back to Freedom now that Blaze and Gia have taken over," he says, staring up at the building.

"Pops told us he just can't leave the kids and youth center. In a way, I understand that. They depend on him, making him feel needed," I say, looking at Hunter.

I see understanding cross his face, and we get out. Sal and three men are standing outside the building waiting for us.

"Hey, Sal." I grin as I approach, fishing my keys from my jeans.

"Hey Mia, ready to show us what you need done?" Sal says.

"Yeah, this one will be much easier than the clubhouse or underground. There won't be structural changes; just renovate and restore," I say, unlocking the door. Sal holds it open as we all enter.

Once inside, I look around, then flip my legal pad open to the list Gia gave me. I don't want to miss anything. I walk them through the main room. "As you can see, it needs a fresh coat of paint throughout the building. I think they're three broken windows that need to be replaced. Everything seems to work in the bathrooms and locker rooms. But you can check them over," I say, looking down at my pad again.

"The same goes for the upstairs apartment. Do fresh paint in standard white, but we should add laminate hardwood throughout and replace the appliances. The new tenant needs it ready as soon as possible. She already signed a lease," I say, looking back at Sal.

"She?" both Sal and Hunter say moving closer. Oops, maybe I should have said them. A woman opening a gym draws attention even though it shouldn't.

"Yes. Now, do you have questions about what needs done?" I ask, looking at Sal, hoping to get back on track.

"No, but if I do, I'll let you know," he says, holding his hand out. Shit, I almost forgot. I slide the key for the building off my key ring, handing it to him.

"Can you text me a timeline in a few days so I can let Gia know?" I ask Sal.

"Sure," he says, and I turn, walking out with Hunter by my side.

After he's through the door, I let it close and get in the van. I run through my head what I need to get done today, but thoughts of Kane and Cowboy keep running keep invading my thoughts. What are they doing right now? Are they really going to get tested like I asked? I feel my cheeks getting warm, remembering how embarrassing that was to ask them. If I'm being honest with myself, part of me wants to be safe, but maybe part of it is I want to wait until I see if they mean what they said before we go further. No matter what my body wants, I need to be logical and protect my heart.

Hunter starts the engine, jerking me from my inner rambling. "Where to next?"

"I need to see the progress on the gas station to update Gia and Axel. Then I need to walk through the apartment complex to make a list of repairs," I say, looking back at Hunter.

He shakes his head as he puts the van into gear. "Damn, girl, you have your hands full with all these projects."

I smile and lean back in my seat, clutching the files to my chest. "I do, and I love it. It keeps me busy and, like Big C, I enjoy feeling needed," I admit.

Hunter glances at me, then stares back out of the windshield. "I can understand that. It probably doesn't hurt that you're earning good money doing it, too," he laughs.

"Nope, that's a definite plus," I grin.

Chapter 5

Kane

I slowly wake up to the sun coming in through the French doors and realize I'm not in my room. I have blackout curtains over my doors. Then I remember holding Mia in my arms last night while Cowboy curled around her body behind her. She fell asleep on my chest, and I swear it was the best fucking night of my life, having my dreamcatcher in my arms. For the first time, I feel complete.

Once she fell asleep on me, I passed out. Damn, I can't remember the last time I slept that good. Burying my face in the pillow, I can still smell her. Where is she? I raise my head, looking over the top of Cowboy, seeing the bathroom doors open. So, she's not in there. Fuck, what time is it?

I lean down and grab my pants, pulling my cell phone out. Shit, it's almost 9 am. I haven't slept this late in years. And I didn't have a nightmare. She is my dreamcatcher. I know she didn't pick up on me calling her that last night. I honestly didn't mean for it to slip out like it did. But I'm not holding back anymore or watching what I say. She needs to know how I feel—all of it.

Cowboy stirs, and I roll onto my back, looking at him.

He opens his eyes, and once they focus, his eyes narrow. "Where is she?"

"Gone," I say, getting up and entering the bathroom. I need to piss and shower. Then, check in with Blaze before getting tested and going by the garage to clean it out. I won't let Mia down, but club business is club business, and I have a clinic to get ready to open.

When I'm finished taking a leak, I enter the bedroom and find my clothes getting dressed. When I grab my socks and boots to head to my room for a quick shower, Cowboy jerks the bathroom door open with such force it hits the wall.

He's holding something in his hand with a disgusted look. "Why the fuck is she taking these?"

I walk over to see what he's holding. I didn't snoop like him. Once I see the packaging and little pills, I know instantly what they are. I take them from him for a closer look. "They're birth control pills," I say. Shit, I don't want her on these. I want a family with her. Raw need to have Mia tied to me in every way rages as I stare back at Cowboy.

His facial expression is angry, telling me he feels the same. We both want her knocked up as soon as possible.

Cowboy takes them from my hand, turns, and enters the bathroom. I follow him, already knowing what he's about to do but needing to confirm it. It's no shock when he holds the package over the toilet and starts popping them out of the foil backing, watching them drop into the water.

"Don't you think we should talk to her about this first?" I ask, knowing this may not end well for us when she sees they're gone.

"Nope, she has no reason to take them. Besides, we are together now. We should discuss all medical decisions."

"I agree with what you're saying, but there are reasons women take them besides to prevent pregnancy," I say, raising a brow. Sometimes, I forget the others don't have the training I do.

Cowboy flushes the toilet, throws the packet in the trash, and then turns towards me. "Ok, know it all. Tell me, why else do women take them?"

"It really depends on the prescription, but birth control can help with regulating periods, reduce cramping, clear their skin up, and for some, it helps prevent migraines," I explain, and his eyebrows raise.

"They teach you that in Medic training?" he asks with a smirk.

"No, smart ass. I read everything I could get my hands on. I considered being a Nurse Practitioner, but nixed that."

Cowboy's eyes widened, but I saw respect in them. "When are you going into the city to get tested?" he asks, walking past me to get dressed.

"After I shower, eat, and check in with Blaze. You coming with?" I ask, walking to the door.

"Hell, yes. I need to set the schedules for the prospects this week, but that won't take long," he says, following me out.

The morning flies by quickly, and we finish up at the clinic. Pissing in a cup and a quick blood draw. It was the 30 minutes in the waiting room I hated, but the 3-day waiting period for results has me grinding my teeth. Fuck, I know I'm clean, but she needs to see it in writing. I'll give her that.

Once we reach the parking lot and straddle our bikes, I pull my cell phone out and dial Hunter. He picks up on the second ring. "Yo, what's up?"

"Hey man, you still with Mia?" I ask. I sure as hell don't want any prospects with her the way they keep flirting. I may have to take them out back and beat their asses before they learn to stay away from her.

"Ya, we've been to the gym and gas station, now we're at the apartments," he replies.

"Fuck," I say, running my hand through my hair. "I appreciate you looking out for her," I say, knowing he has better things to do.

He chuckles. "Don't sweat it; you'd do the same for me. Besides, I needed a change of scenery."

"Ya'll heading back to the clubhouse soon?" I ask, glancing at Cowboy, who is listening closely to my side of the conversation. No doubt, curious about what our woman is doing.

"That's the plan after we leave here," Hunter replies.

"See you there," I say, hitting the end call button and looking at Cowboy. "They're heading back soon," I tell him, and he nods.

After putting on my helmet and starting the engine, I pull out of the parking lot, heading back to Freedom. I need to swing by the Old Dentist's office to see what needs cleaned out, but it is more important to get to the clubhouse before Mia.

I'm not sleeping another night without her. That means I'm moving my shit into her room. She might make a fuss at first, but I'm not going anywhere, and neither is Cowboy. I roll the throttle more, feeling the wind whip past me.

When we pull into the clubhouse lot, I park in my normal spot, remove my helmet, and dismount.

"What's the rush?" Cowboy yells, shutting off his bike.

I throw him a glance over my shoulder. "I'm getting moved in before she gets back."

"Fuck Ya, we are," Cowboy says, following close behind me. "There's no way I'm sleeping without her again. Those days are over."

We march up the steps into the clubhouse, ignoring everyone's stares. We're on a mission. Move in and get comfortable. It hits me. We'll need our dressers in there, too. All our shit won't fit in hers.

"Dressers," I say as we top the staircase and stride down the hall.

"Your room first, then mine. We move everything in," Cowboy says, adjusting his hat and setting his jaw.

Forty-five minutes later, we had everything moved and put away. I was finishing up with my bathroom necessities when I heard Cowboy's voice. "The van's pulling in now," he says, tossing me a smirk. I give him a chin lift and quickly finish putting my shaving gear in the cabinet. I can't wait to see the shock when she realizes we moved in.

I shut the cabinet and head for the door just as Cowboy's swinging it open—time to go down and greet our woman.

Chapter 6

Cowboy

I adjust my hat as I take two stairs at a time to get to Mia. When I reach the main room, I see Mia talking with Bo and Hunter. Our eyes lock as I approach, taking her into my arms and ignoring the others. "Missed you, baby," I say, dipping my head down and capturing those full, delicious lips with mine.

Once I have tasted every inch of her mouth and left her breathless, I pull back, releasing her hips with a grin.

Kane immediately turns her, pulling her into his chest. He threads his fingers into her thick, long hair, and crashes his mouth to hers. I reach down, adjusting myself as I watch him devour her mouth.

They're both panting when they pull away from the kiss, and I wrap my arm around Mia's shoulder. When I look down at her, I see her flushed face, dilated eyes, and heaving chest. Damn, she's so beautiful. I can't wait to have her beneath me. "Have you eaten yet, baby?"

Mia shakes her head no, unable to speak from the lust-induced haze we put her in.

I grin. "Let's get you something to eat." I guide her to the dining room with Kane at her other side. Once we reach our normal table close to the kitchen, I steer her into a chair. "I'll get us some sandwiches."

The prospects only cook breakfast and dinner, so we'll eat sandwiches. I'm not Betty Crocker, but I can do that. Kane gives me a chin lift in thanks and sits next to her. That's when it hits me. With two of us, I won't have to worry when I can't be around. Being V.P. can get hectic sometimes, but I know Kane can be there when I can't.

After making three loaded ham and cheese sandwiches, I grab a bag of chips and head for the table. Mia's deep brown eyes meet mine, and my steps nearly falter. She doesn't even know how beautiful she is.

Setting everything down for us, we eat comfortably. It feels like home when the three of us are together. Kane gets up to get us drinks, and I let my leg rest against hers. Just being near her, touching her in any way I can, is a need I can't describe.

"What are your plans for the day?" I ask her after swallowing the last bite. Mia wipes her mouth with a napkin and grins just as Kane sits back down.

"I'm officially taking the afternoon off to go for a ride. Actually, I want to ride as much as possible so I can get my endorsement fast," she says with a sparkle in her eye. I know she's excited about having her own bike, but part of it is she hates depending on others. Well, she has us now.

"We can all go," I say, glancing over at Kane, who grins from ear to ear.

"Hell, Ya, we will. It's always best to ride in groups anyway," he says, and I nod. I don't want her out there alone. Too many things can happen.

Mia smiles and then raises her hand to her hair. She takes a long lock of it, running her fingers down to the end, which almost reaches her lap. Damn, I love her thick, wavy hair. I bet I could wrap it around my fist real good before plunging into. I'm brought out of my daydream by her next words.

"I need to go to a salon in Wells City soon, too, but not today," she says, which gets my attention.

"What are you wanting to do to your hair?" I ask; every muscle in my body is tense now.

"It's getting too long. If I forget to braid it before bed, it's a tangled mess the next morning." She looks up at me from her hair. Oh no, I sit straighter at that.

"What if I braid it for you at night instead?" Kane asks and my eyes jerk to him. He's staring at me with a raised brow. I'm thinking of tying her to the bed till she changes her mind. What is he thinking?

Mia looks at him skeptically. "Do you know how to braid hair?" she asks him with a laugh.

Kane fakes offense at her question. "Ya, always had it long growing up. I can do a simple braid, just nothing fancy like that French shit you girls do sometimes," he says, and Mia laughs.

When she stops, she tilts her head to the side. "You don't want me to cut it, do you?" she says, looking between us. We both shake our heads no. "Ok then, if you'll braid it for me at night after I shower, I'll hold off on getting it cut."

As soon as she says the words, I feel relief. I reach out, pick her up, and put her on my lap, embracing her tightly. Mia gasps, and I grin. "Good answer baby." I slowly kiss up the side of her face. When I reach her ear, I run my tongue over the outer shell, tasting her soft skin.

"Cowboy," Mia moans, wiggling in my lap, and I tighten my hold on her.

"Yes, baby?" My voice is low as I scrape my teeth over the lobe. Mia groans, wrapping her arms around my neck. When I pull back slightly, her eyes are closed, and her cheeks flushed. Just how I like her, aroused.

I see Kane, out of the corner of my eye, returning from the kitchen. He must have cleaned our mess up. "My turn," he says, taking Mia from my lap and pulling her to him, standing flush against his body. I watch as he runs his hands through her hair, down her back, and over her full plump ass, squeezing it. Damn, he took his time, and I'm enjoying the view.

Bo sits down with a sandwich and grabs the open bag of chips on the table. He smiles watching us. "I didn't know I was getting a show with lunch."

Mia raises a brow. "No one is giving you a show." Bo chuckles and goes back to eating.

I spin Mia and lift her. She squeals, instinctively wraps her legs around my waist, and holds onto my shoulders. "Let's go ride, baby," I say, walking out of the dining room with her.

"My stuff," she says, pointing to the table, and I see a legal pad and files.

"I'll take it to your office," Bo nods.

Kane and I walk out with Mia in my arms. Damn, it's going to feel good riding as a family. It hits me; that's what this is—our first ride as a family. I lower Mia next to her bike and glance at Kane. He's already looking at me with understanding.

We ride for hours all around Freedom. Mia's only had the bike a few days but is a natural. By the end of the week, we'll have her ready to test and get the endorsement she wants.

As we pass by Angel's bar, I have to do a double take and slow down. Her fucking padre is coming exiting as we pass by.

My head jerks in Mia's direction instinctively, and she sees him. The pain I see in her expression nearly undoes me. What the hell is he doing in Freedom? I glance at the road before looking at Kane. The anger rising inside me is reflected in his expression. He is white-knuckling the handlebars, and I nod. We will protect her. There's no reason for him to be in town unless he's looking for her.

Once we get close to the overpass at the edge of town, I ease close to Mia, pointing to the gas station, and she nods. We need to turn around and return to the clubhouse to talk. This isn't good, and I know just seeing him has upset her. No one gets to upset her.

Chapter 7

Mia

Arriving at the overpass on the edge of town, Cowboy eases his bike close and points to the gas station, and I nod, knowing he saw my padre, too. We need to return to the clubhouse and talk.

If my padre is here in Freedom, it can only mean one thing: He's looking for me. There are plenty of bars in Wells City for him to get drunk.

Once we pull into the parking lot, I shut off my bike and dismount. I'm immediately crushed between Kane and Cowboy. My body relaxes, but the worry inside is still raging. I had hoped to never see my padre again and to forget the past. But the past always comes back; I should have known that.

"Are you alright, dreamcatcher?" Kane asks, and I can't hide my smile as I tilt my head back, looking up at him.

"Why do you call me that?" I ask. I mean, I know how he has helped me with my nightmares, but has he had them too?

"Let's go upstairs and talk in private," Kane says, stepping back and taking my hand. Cowboy takes the other, and we walk inside the clubhouse.

As soon as we enter the main room, I see Gia sitting on Blaze's lap watching TV. She turns and looks at us, raising her eyebrows in question at my expression. I shake my head to let her know we'll talk later, and she tilts her head to the side, but my steps don't falter as I follow Kane and Cowboy up the stairs to my room.

When we enter, I stop in my tracks. "Why are there three dressers in here?" Looking around, I notice other things that don't belong to me. Another clock on the nightstand, a couple of pictures, and a helmet on the chair beside the French doors. I walk to the closet seeing my clothes, which are now in the middle, with male clothes on each side. Below, I see boots and tennis shoes neatly arranged beside mine on the floor.

I back out of the closet, shutting the door, my mind racing. They moved in. Turning to face them, my arms crossed over my chest; I raise a brow and wait.

"Mia," Cowboy starts, his voice low and steady. "You're not alone in this anymore."

I glance between them, my eyes lingering on Kane's soft expression. It's a gentleness I haven't seen him show before.

"We moved in because we meant what we said, Mia. We're not going anywhere, ever. You're ours, and we're yours. End of story." Kane's eyes show so much love. Is it possible that he loves me, too? That they both do?

I swallow hard and look between them. "My past is ugly and full of pain. With how things started off between us, it'll take time for me to believe you."

Cowboy steps closer, cupping my face. When I look into his eyes, I see worry, understanding, and, dare I say, love. Tingles spread through me, and my heart skipped a beat.

"You'll see in time. Hell, baby, I'm in love with you. We're in love with you," Cowboy says, his gaze never leaving mine.

Kane steps closer, his hand moving to rest on my shoulder. "We want this life, Mia. We want a family with you."

My heart pounds in my chest. Family. Family and love are all I've ever wanted. To have it with these two amazing men who stole my heart scares me. But the fear that has been gnawing at me starts to fade.

It's replaced with a deep, pulsating desire that sears through my veins as they lean in, their lips meeting each side of my forehead. The tension crackles around us like an electric storm. Their scent - leather mixed with musk and the unmistakable smell of manhood - sends my senses spiraling into overdrive.

"I need to think about how I'm going to deal with my padre," I whisper.

For now, I'm too overwhelmed by the fact they're willing to stake their claim on me and step into the chaotic whirlwind that is my life. And the most frightening part? I want them, too—more than anything else I've ever wanted.

"You're not dealing with it; we are together," Cowboy says, and Kane grunts his agreement, pulling me to sit on the bed with them on each side.

"He doesn't need to come here to drink when they're bars in the city. He's here looking for me," I say as anger and worry course through me. What child wants to confront and deal with an abusive parent? I've defended myself before, but never thought I'd have to again.

I look up, meeting their eyes. "I just want him out of my life. For him to leave me alone so I can be happy." I say, shaking my head. "I never want to see him again."

"He better stay the fuck away from you, or we'll deal with him," Cowboy says through gritted teeth, and I squeeze his hand, loving how protected he makes me feel.

Kane pulls my other hand onto his lap, clasping it between his large, calloused ones, and I look at him. "We won't let him or anyone else hurt you again. I know you're strong, Mia, but you're not alone anymore." Damn, my insides just melted. These two men own my heart, body and soul.

I give them each a warm smile. "Thank you both for everything. I think I want to jump in a hot shower and relax to clear my head," I say, standing.

"Ok, you do that, and I'll grab us all some food and bring it up," Kane says, and I thank him. I would much rather spend the evening with them than downstairs, where everyone is joking and having fun. I'm just not in the mood to deal with people.

I grab a tank top and a pair of sleep shorts since I'm not sleeping alone anymore and go into the bathroom. Starting the shower, I undress and get in as the room fills with steam.

I take my time washing my long hair, enjoying the hot water's relaxing effect. After I rinse and condition it, I lather up my body. My mind wanders over the ride with Kane and Cowboy and how amazing it was. I feel so free when I ride, but having them with me makes it feel complete.

Thinking of them while washing my neck and down over my breasts, my nipples harden into peaks.

I let my hands glide over my body, turning myself on with the thought of Kane and Cowboy's rough hands on me instead. The water splashes against my skin, sending pleasurable shivers down my spine. I close my eyes, choosing to stay in this moment - in the warm embrace of my fantasies.

My hand finds its way down to the apex of my thighs, a soft gasp escaping from between my lips as I become consumed by images: Cowboy's dark, lust-filled eyes boring into mine as he pushes into me; Kane's mouth trailing passionate kisses from my neck down to my chest.

My fingers find my clit, and I circle it with firm pressure as I raise my leg, propping it on the shelf. I lean my back against the wall for support, then cup my breast with my free hand, pinching my nipple.

A loud moan escapes my lips as the thought of their touch becomes too intoxicating. I imagine Cowboy pinning my wrists above my head, his body pressing into mine while Kane devotes his attention to my breasts.

I rock against my fingers, the pleasure mounting with each pass. Thoughts of their bodies entwined with mine, hands exploring every inch of me, mouths claiming and tasting...it's almost too much.

My breath hitching, I allow myself to succumb to the fantasy, a wave of pleasure washing over me as a loud moan escapes from deep within. My legs start to buckle under me from the intensity, but I catch myself against the wall.

I'm jolted from my high as the bathroom door's thrown open. Cowboy comes in, eyes wide. "Are you..." he stops mid-sentence when he sees me through the glass doors panting.

I don't bother covering up as he slides the door open, and his eyes trail up my body. "Fuck, I thought you were hurt," he says, shaking his head. "You clearly don't understand the concept of ours." He growls low and begins stripping.

"Cowboy, what are you doing?"

"Ours means ours. That means to pleasure. If you're in need, we satisfy you," he says, kicking his pants off and laying his cut and hat on the vanity before turning to me.

My eyes trail down, seeing his manhood. Oh my god, he's enormous. My eyes go wide, and my mouth drops open. It's long and thick. There is no way that thing will fit. When he fists it and begins to stroke it, I'm mesmerized for a few minutes as I become aroused all over again. Then my eyes snap up to his.

"Did you get tested?" I ask. I have to know.

"Yes, but we won't get results back for three days," he says with a groan as he steps into the shower with me.

"Then we can't..." Cowboy interrupts me, pinning me to the shower wall and caging me in.

"A lot of things we can do until then, baby. Let me show you," he says, dipping his head down and capturing my mouth with his. When he pushes his massive cock into my stomach and fists my hair, I groan into his mouth.

Suddenly, the door swings open again, and there stands Kane, his brown eyes wide as saucers at the sight of us. "Anybody mind if I join?" he drawls, discarding his clothes onto the floor.

"Come in, brother," Cowboy growls, then steps back for Kane to enter. The shower suddenly feels too small with their towering figures crowding me, but I wouldn't have it any other way.

Kane steps under the stream of water, as his gaze roams over my body. "Seems like I missed quite a bit."

I can feel heat pooling in my core again, my body responding on its own to their intense gazes and the promise of pleasure lingering in the air.

One look at Cowboy's face tells me he's done waiting. He reaches out and traces a finger over my collarbone before dipping down and sucking a nipple into his mouth. I gasp, gripping his biceps for support as delicious shocks of pleasure shoot through me.

Kane's eyes darken as he watches Cowboy, his breath hitching when Cowboy's hands slide down to grip my hips.

He slides a hand between my legs and groans. "Jesus, Mia... you're so wet," Cowboy whispers against my lips before turning to Kane. "Feel for yourself."

My breath hitches as Kane's hand moves between my thighs, his fingers exploring the slick folds of my body. His touch differs from Cowboy's; softer but just as intoxicating. It sends tremors racing down my spine and has me reaching out and gripping his shoulder.

My heart races when Kane drops to his knees and throws my leg over his shoulder, knocking my hand away. I immediately grab his head for support as he dives in.

Chapter 8

Kane

After dropping to my knees, I dive in, sucking Mia's clit into my mouth and inhaling her sweet, intoxicating scent. She's delicious, drawing me in and driving me wild with desire. I hear her gasp above me and feel her fingers digging into my scalp, and it only fuels my need to make her come undone.

Cowboy's moans, mingled with Mia's gasps, fill the steamy air around us. I glance up and see him placing her hand around his shaft, showing her how to stroke him, and the sight makes my cock jerk. Reaching down, I wrap my hand around my shaft and begin taking firm strokes in time with my tongue, devouring Mia's sweet pussy.

While Cowboy is busy pleasing the top half of her body, I'm left to feast on the sweet honey between her thighs.

I lap at her eagerly, swirling my tongue around her swollen clit before dipping lower to plunge my tongue inside her. Her knees buckle, but Cowboy holds her steady, his hands gripping her waist tightly as he continues feasting on her breasts.

I contrast his roughness with tender care, alternating between slow, languid licks and sucking that makes Mia squirm with pleasure. My free hand grips her thigh to steady her, providing just enough leverage for me to delve deeper.

And then it happens; she begins trembling as pleasure courses through Mia, causing her to scream out our names. Her body tenses as she submits to the building orgasm. It crashes through her like an unstoppable wave, and I increase my speed, stroking myself. Our orgasms wash over both of us in hot, heady pulses that leave us reeling.

It's only seconds before Cowboy roars out Mia's name into the room as his hips jerk forward with his release joining us.

When Mia comes down from her high, I gently withdraw my mouth from between her legs and rise to my feet again. Cowboy backs away, his eyes still dark with desire but a satisfied smile on his lips.

I tenderly lean down, kissing Mia, and whisper, "I love you." When I pull back, Mia cups my face with her hands and looks into my eyes with such intensity my heart nearly stops. "I love you, Kane."

Fuck, those words on her lips mean everything. I grab her and plant a hard, demanding kiss. A claim that she's mine.

When I step back to grab the shower gel and a washcloth to clean her, she does the same to Cowboy. She cups his face and looks at him with the same emotional, love-filled eyes she did me moments ago.

"I love you, Cowboy," she says and gets on her tiptoes. Cowboy picks her up into his arms and kisses the hell out of her, making me chuckle. I know that feeling of being overwhelmed by hearing her say those words.

When he sits her down, I hand him a washcloth with a knowing smile. We begin washing our woman—our future wife and mother of our children.

We take our time enjoying touching her and exploring Mia's curvy body as we wash her. Once we're done, she grabs the shower gel and does the same for us. Exploring and caressing with her whole hands, letting her fingers glide over us.

Her eyes follow as she explores, and it hits me. "We're the first men you've seen or touched," I say, hoping like hell I'm right. But also knowing I have no right to judge her if we aren't.

Mia's face flushes again, and she nods. Her gaze stays on my chest as she pushes me back under the water to rinse off, not meeting my eyes.

We get out, and Cowboy begins drying her amazing body. I take a towel to dry her hair. Once I'm finished, I take the brush and remove any tangles before braiding it. Mia smiles at me in the mirror, and I grin back. We both remember my promise to do this each night so it doesn't get knotted when she sleeps.

I groan when she puts on a tank top and shorts, hating that she's covering up.

"Why are you getting dressed?" Cowboy growls in disapproval, and I nod in agreement, not liking it.

Mia turns when she's dressed and grins at us. "Because our sexual tension is already through the roof. I'm hoping this will help until the results are back and we're ready to do more."

I groan, shoving my hand through my wet hair, knowing damn well she's right. It will make it a little easier to control ourselves if she's not sleeping naked.

I step forward, taking her by the waist and pulling her to me. Mia places her hands on my chest to brace herself. "Make no mistake, dreamcatcher, as soon as those results are back these," I say, pulling the edge of her top between my fingers. "Will not be coming to bed with us again."

Mia visibly swallows hard but nods in agreement, making me smirk. She better agree, or I'd throw them away.

Mia steps back, picks up her toothbrush, puts toothpaste on it, and brushes her teeth. Cowboy and I do the same when I see Mia pause mid-stroke, pulling the toothbrush out of her mouth.

"Where is my birth control?" she asks, pointing at the counter, and I glance at Cowboy before looking back at her.

"We threw it away," I state as a matter of fact.

Mia's eyes widened in surprise, and the toothbrush fell from her hand to clatter into the sink. "You did what?"

"We threw it away," I repeat calmly, trying to keep my pulse steady, even as the intensity in Mia's eyes sends it racing.

"But why..." she began, only to be cut off by Cowboy stepping forward.

"Because we can't wait to put a baby in you, Mia. Fuck, we want everything with you," he says, cupping her face.

I step to her side, taking her chin between my fingers and making her look at me. "It takes time to get out of your system, but Mia, we want it all with you." I place a hand on her stomach. "The thought of you carrying our child drives me crazy." It's another way of claiming her, but how do I make her understand that?

There was a stunned silence in the room as Mia digested my words. Her eyes flickered back and forth between us, her mouth opening and closing without uttering a word. Then, finally, she spoke.

"OK, but you guys just can't decide for me like that. We have to talk," she says, pointing between us.

I nod, but in my mind, I know the truth. I would convince her no matter what it took. Like giving her so many orgasms, she passed out or agreed, I think to myself.

We go into the room and eat our cold pizza. Thankfully, none of us mind it cold. There's a knock at the door as we sit, talking about each other's day.

I immediately pulled the sheet over my lap, and Cowboy did the same since we were only in our boxers. Mia got off the bed and answered it.

When she opens it, I'm surprised to see Blaze and Gia standing in the hall, and I stiffen.

"What's up?" Mia asks, glancing between them.

"We just wanted to check in with you guys," Gia says, studying Mia. "You all looked upset when you came back from your ride."

Mia steps to the side, opening the door wider for them to enter. When Mia closes the door, she crosses her arms over her chest, and the action raises her breasts, making me groan. Damn, she isn't wearing a bra.

"We were riding past Angel's bar and saw my padre coming out of it," she says, looking from Gia to Blaze.

"That son of a bitch," Gia yells, and Blaze wraps his arms around her.

Mia nods. "There's only one reason for him to be in Freedom, and we all know what that is. Me."

"How do you want us to handle it?" Blaze asks Mia, I'm sure wanting to be considerate of her feelings. But we all just want to kill the bastard for what he's done to her. Especially since getting his ass kicked didn't do the trick.

Mia shakes her head at Blaze. "Let us handle it," Mia says, gesturing to me, and Cowboy making me smirk.

"Mia's ours to protect. We'll be claiming her in church as soon as she accepts," I say, staring at Blaze. He gives me a firm nod in understanding and looks at Cowboy.

"She's ours; I'll be claiming her too," Cowboy says, leaving no room for argument.

"You heard them. Now, we need to let them deal with it," Blaze says, looking down at Gia. Her expression tells me she doesn't like it, but she nods.

Gia looks at Mia with a warm, motherly look. "You know where to find me if you want to talk."

Mia smiles stepping forward, hugging her. "Thank you."

Once they leave, Mia locks the door and returns to bed. As soon as she's close, I grab her, tossing her to the middle between us—time to hold our woman and get some sleep.

"You didn't tell me why you call me dream catcher," she whispers, and I grin into her hair.

"Because you stop the nightmares," I say honestly.

"Neither did I last night. I think you and Cowboy stop mine too," she says, and I mold my body tighter against her back and kiss her head.

Cowboy throws his leg over Mia and me and getting closer. "Goodnight, family," is the last thing I hear before drifting off to sleep.

Chapter 9

Cowboy

I can't help but enjoy stealing glances at Mia as we eat breakfast. My hand rests on her thigh while Kane's arm is around her shoulder. The sexy smile on her face as she eats makes me want to take her back upstairs for a repeat of last night's fun. But I know I need to take things slow until we get our results back. A groan escapes me at the thought, and Mia looks at me quizzically while Kane tosses a knowing look.

I give Mia a slow smile and then look over at Kane. "You going to the old dentist's office today to clean it out?"

He nods and swallows. "Yeah, if you go with Mia to check on the other sites today, you can meet me there after."

I give him a chin lift in response and look down at her. "Where are we going, baby?" I ask with a grin.

Mia takes a drink and then slides her legal pad closer to look. "I have to go by the Underground to ensure they're ready for opening night. Then, stop by the gym to see how Sal is coming along. Next is the apartment complex walk-through. I have to make a list of renovations to be done. Last is meeting Kane to see what he wants done for the clinic," she says.

"Damn, that's a full day," I say with a raised brow.

Mia shakes her head and laughs. "Nope, it will leave the late afternoon free for a ride and some fun."

I groan and squeeze her thigh. My idea of fun doesn't include riding bikes. Mia's eyes go wide, and her cheeks flush. Humm, is my baby getting aroused thinking of all the fun we could have? Kane leans down, whispering in her ear, making her face go from flushed to red, and she nods.

Fuck, whatever he said, I'm all in, and so is my now rising dick. I take my free hand, reach down to readjust it to a more comfortable position and catch Kane doing the same. He tasted her last night; I will eat my fill tonight.

Kane kisses her and leaves. Mia gathers her things, and then we mount our bikes. I really want her wrapped around me. Maybe after she gets over the newness of having her own bike, she'll ride with me.

By the time we finish everything on her list, including inspecting the whole damn apartment building, which is trashed, it's 2 pm. I'm hungry and tired already, so Mia has to be.

We walk out to the parking lot, stopping next to our bikes, and I put my arms around her, pulling her close. Dipping my head down, I inhale the floral scent of her shampoo deeply while I hold her to my chest. That curvy body of hers pushing into mine is pure heaven.

"You hungry, baby?" I ask, looking into her big brown eyes.

"Starved, you?" she says.

"Yeah, why don't we grab some food and eat with Kane?" I ask.

"Great idea. Burgers?" she asks with a hopeful look, and I laugh. Fuck, I would give her anything. We ride into the edge of Wells City and hit a drive-thru for burgers and a gas station for drinks.

I hold the door open for Mia as we exit the gas station. We don't make it three steps before Mia suddenly stops and has a scowl. I follow her line of sight and see her padre walking right toward us with a serious expression. I immediately step closer to her, but slightly in front to protect her. When I reach the bag of drinks to her so I can kick his ass. Mia pushes it away, shaking her head. "It's time I handled this once and for all." Her voice is bitter, like I've never heard, and she squares her shoulders. I sit the bag down as her padre gets close.

When he stops in front of us, I first notice that he looks sober, and then I see the remorse and sadness in his eyes. Shit, it's too late for all that after what he's done to her.

"Mia, can we talk?" he says, glancing from her to me with a worried look. He better be worried, I think, as anger rushes through me at the sight of him.

Mia stiffens, and her expression hardens. "What would you like to talk about?" she spits. "How you beat me for years? The fact I grew up afraid to sleep? Or how you were a drunk who blew his money and never put food in the house?" she says, her voice rising with each word. People stop and watch their interactions, pointing.

"I..." He begins, but Mia interrupts him.

"No! You don't get to speak." Her chest heaves with emotions - rage, hurt, betrayal. I clench my fists at my sides, every protective instinct screaming for me to intervene. But this moment is hers, I remind myself. I'll step in if he makes a move.

Her padre's face crumbles, the remorse in his eyes replaced by a fear he should've been feeling years ago. He's lost his daughter. "Mia, I'm..."

"No!" Mia approaches him and brings her face dangerously close to his. "You're nothing to me now. You stopped being my padre a long time ago. I have no padre."

He nods sadly and slinks away without another word.

Standing under the hot sun, Mia watches him walk across the parking lot. Her hands shake as she lets them fall to her sides. Without a word, I take her into my arms as she breaks down, sobbing into my chest.

"Shhh...," I say into her hair as I stroke her back.

After several minutes, Mia pulls away, looking up at me with tear-filled eyes. "I'm sorry you had to see that," she whispers, wiping her cheeks.

Her apology stills me. "Don't be sorry, baby," I say, my voice gruff with emotion. "You've got nothing to apologize for."

She gave me a small smile as she picked up the bag of drinks. Neither of us said anything as we mounted our bikes to meet Kane.

Pulling up outside what will be Freedom Clinic on Main Street, I drop my kickstand and look around, shutting the engine off. I've ridden by here hundreds of times but never looked at it as an outsider. These empty shops really have potential. In a few years, this really could be a thriving town—hell, maybe sooner.

I look at Mia, who has been watching me with a smile. "You see it now, don't you?" she asks with a knowing look.

"Ya, it's crazy how I never took the time to realize it before," I say, getting off my bike and removing our lunch from the saddlebags.

Mia takes her helmet off and walks to my side. "We all talk about it every day. But we don't take the time to envision it. But I see it," she says, looking down the street. "I see what it will look like once we're done."

Damn, the look of awe and wonder on her face, along with her intelligence makes her even more beautiful. Gia picked the perfect person for the town planner. And I am one lucky son of a bitch to have Mia as my woman. No way am I screwing that up.

Kane comes out of the building, pulling me from my thoughts. He scoops Mia into his arms and twirls her around. She throws her head back, and her laughter rings out into the air.

"Hey, hey!" I protest, feigning jealousy. "I thought you were supposed to be working." I laugh.

Kane chuckles, placing Mia back down on her feet. "Well, the place isn't going to clean itself out now, is it?" He glances at the bags in my hands. "I see you brought lunch."

We go inside and sit on stools behind the old receptionist counter. As I watch Kane and Mia interact—the easy camaraderie between them laced with flirting, something I'm a part of—I can't help but think about how lucky we all are.

Kane looks at me with raised eyebrows. "Something was on your mind earlier; I could see it on your face."

I nod, knowing he can read me easily after all these years. I look at Mia to see if she wants to tell him about our run-in with her padre, and she nods. My eyes never leave Kane as she tells him everything. A wide range of emotions cross over his face. The last two were clear: sadness for Mia and anger towards her padre. Mia takes his hand and squeezes it. "It's over now. I'll never speak to him again."

After we finish eating, Mia insists on seeing the entire building. We follow her through each room, littered with old dentist equipment and furniture. Despite the dust and clutter, I can visualize what it will look like once we fix it up.

"I'll need your measurements," Mia says to Kane, looking around. "And we'll need to decide on a layout before renovating."

"You think you can turn this dump into a clinic?" I ask, trying to instigate.

Mia turns around and fixes me with a stern gaze. But there's a glint in her eye. "I know I can." And damn, it makes me want her even more.

The rest of our afternoon is spent measuring and doing some heavy lifting as we clear out anything that can't be used in the clinic. By 5 p.m., we're finished.

I walk up behind Mia, wrapping my arms around her waist and pulling her into my hard body. "Ready to go for that ride, baby?" She tilts her head back and gives me the biggest smile that makes my heart skip a beat.

"I say we go for a ride, then head back to the clubhouse. We have some orange cones we can set up for her to practice maneuvers," Kane says, grabbing his helmet.

"Yes," Mia chirps. It sounds good to me. We can drink beers and watch her. A glance at Kane tells me he had the same thought.

"Sounds like a plan," I say, leading her outside by her waist. Mia hops onto her bike with so much excitement that I can't help but grin. It's infectious.

We take the long way to the clubhouse, winding through the streets and letting Mia get a feel of the roads. I watch her in my rearview mirror, her body moving as she leans into the turns, fearless as she picks up speed. The woman is a natural adrenaline junkie, and it makes my blood pump harder.

Once we reached the clubhouse, we set up an obstacle course with orange cones. Mia's eyes dance with challenge at the sight.

"Alright," Kane starts, rubbing his hands together. "Let's see what you've got."

Mia playfully revs her bike before setting off on the course, weaving through the cones with admirable ease for a first-timer. Kane and I stand at a safe distance, leaning against his truck as we nurse our beers and enjoy the view.

"She's good," Kane remarks, bringing his beer to his lips. "Real good."

"I know," I respond, unable to hide the pride in my voice. "She's something else."

Mia finishes her run and circles back toward us, grinning. She parks her bike next to ours and removes her helmet, letting her hair tumble free. I'll never know how she tucks all that hair inside it.

"So? How'd I do?" She asks.

"Perfect," I reply, earning myself an appreciative smirk from Kane. "No. I think you're ready to take your test and get your motorcycle endorsement on your license." I look over at Kane, who is nodding his agreement.

Mia dismounts and lays her helmet down. "I have a lot to do again tomorrow. Maybe I can go the day after."

Shoving my cowboy hat back further on my head, I have her in my arms, pulling her to me in two long strides. She runs her hands up my chest and wraps her arms around my neck. "Kane and I have to return to Wells City anyway, so we'll all go. We can celebrate after," I say with a smirk.

Mia cocks her head to the side with a grin, then it hits her what I'm saying. We get our results back then. Claiming her will be one hell of a celebration.

Kane comes up behind her, grasping her hips and grinding himself into her, making her moan.

He leans close to her ear and growls loud enough for the three of us to hear. "Are you ready to be claimed dreamcatcher? Owned and claimed by your men?"

Mia's breathing picks up, and she tilts her head back, looking up at him with wide, dilated eyes and flushed cheeks. "Yes," she says, then looks up at me. Her little pink tongue comes out, running across her bottom lip, and fuck me, I can't take it.

I throw her over my shoulder in a fireman's carry, making her squeal in surprise and Kane chuckles. Slapping her on the ass, I say, "Shower then, dessert, baby."

She puts her hands on my ass, trying to push her body up as I take long, determined strides through the main room of the clubhouse and up the stairs. "What do you mean, dessert?" she asks with a laugh, and I hear Kane groan.

When I reach the door to our room, I open it rougher than intended and then sit her down. I grasp her face with both hands and stare into her eyes. "I mean, I need to taste that sweet pussy, baby. So, we're showering, then I'm going to eat until you beg me to stop." I turn her towards the bathroom that Kane is already in, naked and has the shower going, waiting for us with a broad grin and a hard-on that could pound nails.

Chapter 10

Mia

I'm a mess by the time Kane and Cowboy finish washing me and themselves. Their hands were all over me, teasing me to no end. I can't take it anymore and get out drying off. Cowboy scoops me up into the air as I reach for the hairbrush with a growl. "I need to taste you now," he says, and I press my thighs together, trying to ease my aching core.

He lays me on the bed, flipping me over, and grasps my hips. "Hands and knees, baby. I want you to ride my face."

What? I think, but my hungry vagina is screaming hell, yes. Cowboy lies on the bed, motioning for me to straddle his face. I do, and he pulls me down onto him with force. I squeak in surprise and brace my hands on the bed as he takes a long lick that sends pleasure coursing through me.

Kane steps beside the bed in front of me, stroking his massive cock. His eyes look down at me with a hunger that has my nipples painfully hard. The overwhelming intensity consumes me as I stretch out my hand, beckoning Kane to come closer. As he moves nearer, the look of raw desire in his eyes is intoxicating.

Cowboy's hands on my hips guide me to move against him, his tongue delving deeper with each stroke, flicking and sucking.

Kane kneels on the edge of the bed next to me, his erection hard and ready between us. I wrap my hand around it. He places his large hand over mine, guiding me to grip him hard and move faster.

Cowboy's tongue continues its relentless assault on my senses, flicking and teasing, drawing moans from deep within me. As Kane groans out, "Mia."

I arch my back higher, begging for more, while Kane's hips buck into my hand. Cowboy growls low in his throat. "You ready to come for us, baby?" His voice is thick with lust as he inserts a finger into my entrance.

My body instinctively clamps down on him, and he groans. When he curls his finger, hitting a spot that has my eyes rolling back into my head, I gasp. The sound spurs Cowboy to renew his assault, his lips, teeth and tongue devouring me with an intensity that threatens to drive me mad. Kane removes his hand as I take faster strokes, determined to take him over the edge with me. He tangles his fingers in my hair, gripping it tight, and the pinch of pain feels amazing. Cowboy starts rocking beneath me, and I know he's stroking himself. The three of us are chasing our orgasms.

Cowboy increases his pace, and I cry out as pleasure coursing through me.

"God, Mia," Kane grunts out between clenched teeth, his fingers digging into my hair as he thrusts harder. "So, fucking good."

My eyes roll back into my head, and cries escape my lips at the waves of pleasure tearing through me. Each ripple grows stronger until I scream out my release.

My vision fades, and my body trembles with the force of it. A warmth spreads over my back just as Cowboy yells, "Fuck!" His warm release comes in pulses, hitting my back.

Kane groans, and thick jets of white come shoot onto my breast. He tries to hold us both up with the intensity of it all. Our eyes lock, and the love I see in his has my heart ready to beat out of my chest.

Kane grabs my face with both hands, crashing his lips onto mine. Holding onto his arms for support, I return the kiss, massaging my tongue with his. When we pull away, Cowboy slides from beneath me, taking me into his arms and sitting me on his lap.

"Damn baby, I love you so much," he says, claiming my mouth. We kiss until we're out of breath.

"Shower time again," Kane says, and Cowboy lifts me, carrying me back into the bathroom. We don't waste any time cleaning up.

When we're done, they lead me to the bed, and I crawl to the center, getting beneath the covers. Kane on one side and Cowboy on the other hold me tight. I notice them staring at each other for a long time, as if silently communicating.

Then Kane looked at me with a serious expression. "Tomorrow, we all go into Wells City. You take your test, so that's out of the way, and then we'll get our test results."

I nod because that all sounds wonderful to me. Cowboy grasps my chin between his thumb and forefinger, turning me to face him. "Mia, we aren't going any further with you until you agree to be ours and only ours. It's time we claimed you in church."

"I've always been yours, both of yours," I say, looking between them. "The only thing holding us back was you two being stupid," I say with a smirk. But my pulse is pounding in my ears. I've wanted them both since we met.

"You're right," Cowboy admits, tracing the curve of my hip beneath the sheet. "We were being stupid."

Kane's brow arches in mock offense. "Stupid, huh?" His voice is a low rumble, the corners of his mouth quirking upwards into that irresistible grin I love. Cowboy snorts from behind me, his laughter vibrating my back and adding another layer of warmth to our tangled bodies.

"Guess we deserved that," Kane murmurs, his grip tightening around me. His lips graze the sensitive skin of my neck, igniting a trail of goosebumps in their wake. "You stay comfortable while Cowboy and I go downstairs to grab dinner."

"We're eating up here again?" I ask, sitting higher on the bed and resting my back against the headboard.

"Yeah, well, call us selfish," Cowboy says, pulling on his jeans and zipping them up. "We like you all to ourselves."

Kane chuckles as he dresses, then pushes his long hair out of his face. "If we had our way, you'd never leave this room." My mouth drops open at his words, knowing damn well that wouldn't be happening. His lip lifts in amusement as they walk out of the door. I grin, leaning my head back. There may be two of them, but they have no idea how stubborn and independent I've become.

Chapter 11

Kane

I'm jolted awake with a smack to my face and see Mia fast asleep, softly snoring. I grin at my dreamcatcher, whose face is inches from mine. She must have been reaching for me in her sleep. I lean forward, kiss her head, and slide out of bed. The sooner we get into Wells City, the faster we have those results. The need to claim Mia in church, physically, hell, making her mine in every way possible has my blood pumping.

I grab jeans and a T-shirt, get dressed, and then rush into the bathroom. I'll wake Mia up while Cowboy gets ready, knowing he will be as eager as I am. Damn, I never thought I could have this amazing life or a family, for that matter. Now that it's in my grasp and happening, I feel alive again.

Once I'm finished, I enter the bedroom, nudging Cowboy awake. He groans, peeling his heavy lids open. "We need to head out. Today's the day," I say, and his eyes widen before he kisses Mia's head, jumping up. He loves her as much as I do; it's written all over him. I settle on the bed beside Mia, leaning over and stroking her cheek. "Time to wake up, dreamcatcher."

Her eyes flutter open, and she looks at me before a slow smile forms. She rises, pressing her naked body against me, and I groan, wrapping my arms around her. "You need to get ready, baby; it's test day for all of us."

Mia kisses my chest and climbs out of bed with a broad smile.

We arrive in Wells City by 9 a.m. Mia's excitement is palpable as we enter the DMV. After registering for the tests, surprisingly, both the written and driven parts only take 2 hours for her to complete.

She strolls back into the building, triumphant at passing, and 15 minutes later, she's clutching her new license like it's the most important thing in the world. It's a step of independence for her–a symbol of freedom–and my chest swells with pride at her accomplishment.

She disappears into the restroom, and Cowboy and I wait patiently in the waiting room, the seconds ticking slower than usual.

Suddenly, there's a commotion inside the restroom, along with a muffled scream that has my blood running cold. It's Mia.

Without thinking, I run down the hallway, blasting through the bathroom door, Cowboy at my heels. Three men have Mia cornered against the grimy bathroom wall. She fights like a wildcat, kicking and flailing, but they overpower her.

My fists are flying before I even register what I'm doing. One connects with a man's jaw in a satisfying crack, while Cowboy's boot lands with a sickening crunch on the kneecap of the second. The bathroom echoes with their pained howls, drowned out by the roar of blood rushing through my ears.

Everything in me calms when I see the third man pulling a knife from his pocket. I'm a trained killer, and he just fucked up. First, by touching what's mine. Second, for pulling a weapon on me. But Mia is quicker. She grabs a mop from leaning in the corner, swinging it down like an axe with an enraged scream. The wooden handle connects with the man's hand, skittering the knife across the restroom floor.

Cowboy and I are on him in seconds, slamming him into the wall. Our fists pummel him relentlessly until he crumbles onto the floor, unconscious. We stand over him, our chests heaving with exertion and relief.

"Are you okay?" I ask Mia, grabbing her by the shoulders and crushing her to my chest. Her eyes are wide but determined as she nods, fisting my cut.

"I'm fine," she breathes out. "Thanks to you two. I couldn't take on all three." Cowboy comes to her back, wrapping his arms around her waist and kissing her head repeatedly.

The door flies open, and a short older woman from the DMV bursts in. "What's going on in here?" she says, taking in the sight of three unconscious men on the floor.

Trying to think fast, I say, "Just a family squabble." I remember they have cuts on, too, and most civilians ignore the colors.

"Leave and take them with you, or I'm calling the police," she says with a huff, walking out. I nod, looking at Cowboy with a smirk. He returns it, pulling his phone from his jeans and dialing Blaze. We drag the three men out the back entrance, then retrieve our bikes from the front and wait. Thirty minutes later, Hunter, Blaze, and three others are here with the van, loading them up to return to the clubhouse.

On the way back, Mia rides with me. Halfway there, she squeezes my waist tighter and yells over the sound of the engine and wind whipping around us. "Did you notice the largest man's name on his cut?"

Fuck, I didn't take the time to read names. The only thing that grabbed my attention while we waited for our brothers to arrive was that they were Diablo's. Filthy bastards, I think, gripping the handlebars tighter. I shake my head no. Mia presses herself against my back and yells, "Sgt. at arms," I grin. Torturing him for information is going to be fun. He fucked up, laying his hands on my woman. I glance over at Cowboy riding alongside us, and his face is firm when he gives me a chin lift. His expression shows the same determination as mine. We're going to introduce those assholes to what pain is.

Rolling on the throttle harder, it isn't long before we pull into the clubhouse parking lot. Excitement races through me at inflicting pain on them for touching Mia. I have to know why they did it. Taking Mia's hand in mine while Cowboy takes her other hand. He puts his cowboy hat in place, and we all go to the parking van. My blood is pumping as the doors open and my brothers exit. I release Mia's hand. "Go inside, baby," I say, but she gives me a hard, defiant look.

"It was me they attacked and said I was coming with them. I'm not missing this. I think I deserve to know what they intended to do with me before I have my fun," she says with an evil grin, and I swear my dick just doubled in size. She's hot as fuck when she's mad.

"You got it, dreamcatcher." I grin and look at Cowboy. His face is stone cold, but he can't hide that Mia just made him hot, too, with her statement.

I reach out, jerking the back doors open, and Cowboy steps to my side. Our fellow Outcasts gather around, including prospects, to see what we hauled back. No doubt already knowing what happened. I grab the biggest mother fucker of the group, who Mia said, was their Sgt. at arms dragging him to the edge. Sure enough, that's what's on his cut, along with Grave Digger. I chuckle darkly at reading it and look over at Cowboy. "The only grave he's dug today is his own," I say, hoisting him over my shoulder in a fireman's carry and marching towards the clubhouse.

Cowboy chooses the next one, Blaze takes the last. It's time to get information, then take out the trash.

Chapter 12

Cowboy

With a swift motion, I throw one of Mia's attackers over my shoulder. We march with determined strides into the clubhouse, through the main room, and straight for the basement entrance. Gia is standing in the hallway with the door already open for us. The cold, hard look on her face is one I've only seen on her in the ring as Rebel. She wants blood for what they've done as much as we do.

Following Kane down the steps, I hear a stampede behind me. It's not surprising, given that Blaze is carrying the third man, and Gia and my brothers want in on this.

When we reach the bottom, we turn to the far right. Kane, Blaze, and I toss them to the floor like trash. I look up and see Gia and Bo opening the doors to the Armory. It was the wedding gift they received from her Nonno. I chuckle, remembering their faces when he showed them the inside of the truck filled with various weapons and ammo.

As I look down at the men on the floor, my fists clench while I read each of their cuts: Sgt. at arms, prospect, prospect.

"Fuckers," I utter with venomous hatred. I watch them through narrowed eyes as they regain consciousness.

Mia moves forward with confidence that morphs into something far more deadly. She stops in front of the table Gia and Bo have placed weapons on. Mia picks up a baseball bat, gripping it by the end and letting the length drop to the floor. She returns to the largest man, Grave Digger, and stops with an evil grin.

He takes in his surroundings with confusion, but it morphs into fear, seeing all of us. "Welcome to hell," I growl before delivering a swift kick to his gut. He groans, curling in on himself, and pain contorts his features.

"Who sent you?" The question leaves my lips just as Mia steps closer, raising the bat to her shoulder. Her eyes have a spark of violence. Grave Digger looks her over and chuckles, making my blood boil.

"I was sent to get you," he says with a crooked smile, revealing his disgusting yellow teeth. "But I wouldn't mind having some fun with you before handing you over to Diablo."

Blaze grabs him, standing him up, and I throw a punch to his jaw. The satisfying crack that follows is music to my ears. Kane lands a blow to his ribs that has all the air rushing from his lungs. I want to continue, but we need more answers. "Why does Diablo want Mia?" I ask through clenched teeth. It's taking everything I have to restrain myself at this moment.

Grave Digger is having trouble breathing through the pain already, which is pathetic. After he turns his head and spits, his eyes focus on my woman. "You were the easiest to get to," he says with a smirk before looking at us, pausing at Blaze. "You and your bitch fucked with our money. Our orders were to fuck with you. Take one of your women as leverage. Gia was harder to get to and had heavier consequences, so Mia was the best choice. Her going off alone to take a piss was the perfect opportunity to grab her." The malicious laugh that follows has my blood boiling. Son of a bitch, we're ending all of them.

"My turn," Mia says, stepping forward with the bat pushing between Kane and me. She brings the bat down and hits him in the kneecap. His pain-filled scream is music to my ears, echoing through the room. She hits his other one for good measure, and he crumples.

I see her hesitate for a heartbeat before she steps forward again. Raising the bat and bringing it around hard, a visceral crack rings out as it connects with his jaw. His head snaps back from the impact, blood spraying out over the floor in a gruesome arc.

"Who else is involved?" she asks, bringing herself to eye level with him as he writhes on the floor. "Every. Single. Name."

He spits, making blood and teeth fly from his mouth onto the concrete floor. "Fuck you," he grits out, glaring up at Mia with pure hatred in his eyes.

I shake my head, a feral grin spreading across my face as my hand wraps around hers, taking the bat. I kneel, wrap my other hand around his throat, and tighten my grip.

"No, fuck you," my voice was low and deadly as I put pressure on his larynx.

His eyes bulge as I continue to squeeze, his hands clawing against my grip. Then, just like that, I release him. He gasps for breath, clutching at his bruised throat.

"Tell me what we want to know." I grit out.

The room is silent except for Grave Digger's harsh gasps for air. His eyes look wild, but I can see the flicker of fear as he nods.

He spits out Diablo, followed by the mayor of Wells City, and Gia gasps and steps forward. Blaze is at her side within seconds. "The mayor and Diablo are still doing business?" Gia fists a handful of his hair and jerking his head to look at her.

"Never stopped," Grave Digger says with a cough, and Gia shoves him away, standing and looking at Blaze with such fierceness that it's chilling. "We're calling Sammy and Nonno to deal with him. Wells City is their domain," she says. Then she turns to us, looking from Mia to Kane, then to me. "I'll get the incinerator ready for when you're done."

I give her a chin lift in thanks as Mia walks to the side wall where Bo is leaning against it. She joins him, ready to watch. Kane and I move in unison, beating all three of them until they are unconscious, before tossing and loading them into the incinerator for disposal. They answered a few more questions. We now know the layout of their clubhouse, the number of members, and the weapons at their disposal. It's information we wouldn't have gotten otherwise.

While Kane and I take our woman upstairs, the others stay to finish things. Today didn't turn out like I thought it would. I hold Mia's hand tight as we approach our room. Claiming her is always on my mind, but now isn't the time after the attack. We still haven't gotten our test results. Tonight, we take care of her; tomorrow, we'll worry about the rest. A glance at Kane tells me his mind is in cinque with mine. Tomorrow, we take care of the other shit; our woman takes priority.

Mia, trembling with the adrenaline fading from her body, allows Kane and I to guide her through the door of our room. Her beautiful eyes hold a mix of emotions, determination and pride. She's been through hell today, but it's only made her stronger. Our woman is a badass.

"I'm okay," she assures us as we help her sit on the edge of the bed. Her voice is steady despite everything.

I kneel before her, cradling her face in my hands. "We need to strip you down, baby," I say, tracing her cheekbone with my thumb. "Need to see you... make sure you're okay."

Mia gives us a slight nod, granting permission. Carefully, we undress her. Each piece of clothing that falls feels like unwrapping a precious gift. Her skin is like silk against my hands as I glide them over her, needing to touch her everywhere.

She has bruises - blotches of blue and black, marring her silky skin. Those motherfuckers' rough hands left them, and I growl at the sight.

"We'll make it better, dreamcatcher," Kane rasps beside me, echoing my thoughts. He takes one hand, and I take the other, leading her into the bathroom. Kane and I undress and start the shower.

Our hands are firm yet gentle as they skim across the exposed flesh. Mia shivers beneath our touch as we wash her. Kane shampooing her hair, and I take care of her body. A tremor runs through her as my soapy hands roam over her curves, exploring every inch. But this isn't about lust; this is about Mia knowing she's cared for and loved.

After we're clean and relaxed, Kane braids her hair while I jog downstairs. I order the prospects to put together a picnic for three. I have a plan. Our woman needs the rest of her day to be relaxing. A ride and picnic will relax us all.

Chapter 13

Mia

Slowly waking up, I stretch and reach out for Kane and Cowboy. My eyes jerk open, realizing they aren't here, but the bed is still warm. They haven't been gone long. Then it hits me. They're doing one of two things: getting breakfast or riding into Wells City to get their test results. Sitting up and sliding out of bed, I get dressed, remove my long braid, and brush it out.

Studying my face in the mirror, I see only one slight bruise forming on my jaw. It should fade fast. I inspect my arms, and the fingerprints those assholes left will be there awhile. Nasty blues and purples are clear as day; I sigh, shaking my head. I'm glad it was me instead of Gia they tried to take. Once I'm satisfied with the natural waves and curls, I finish my morning routine before jogging downstairs.

When I reach the last step, I see Kane and Cowboy talking to Hunter and Hawk. I walk closer and listen as they order them to ensure I'm not alone until they return from Wells City. So I was right. I grin, walking closer.

But before I reach them, they turn, going into the dining room. I follow with a smile. They are former military and don't know I'm behind them. I have to hold back a laugh as Cowboy and Kane approach Blaze and Gia. What they say next has me stopping in my tracks.

"We need you to order Mia's cut. We're claiming her in church," Cowboy says, and Kane nods.

"She agrees to you claiming her?" Blaze asks, and Gia elbows him, making a smirk appear on Blaze's face. "Gotta ask," he says.

"Ya, she's ours," Kane says, and Blaze stands slapping him on the back, congratulating him. His eyes flick to me, and he smiles. But I can't move from my spot; excitement and happiness envelop me like I've never felt before. It's happening.

Cowboy and Kane turn to see what Blaze is looking at, and their eyes meet mine. I stand still with a broad smile, not knowing what to say. Cowboy instantly has me in his arms, possessive and protective, as always. He crushes his lips to mine, stealing my breath away. "You're ours, baby. Always been."

Kane approaches from behind me, wrapping his arms around my waist, his rough fingers tracing over the bruises on my arm. His voice is firm in my ear, echoing Cowboy's words, "We're claiming you, dreamcatcher. You are ours."

His deep baritone voice sends a thrill coursing through me, and I can feel my heart pounding.

Finally finding my voice, I whisper. "And you're mine." Their faces light up, hearing my words. There's a cheer from the Outcasts pouring into the dining room as they watch us.

Cowboy's husky voice cuts through the noise. "Let's get our woman something to eat before we ride out."

My stomach growls its approval at his words, and Kane chuckles low in his throat as he brushes some stray hair away from my face. His dark eyes sparkle with mischief when he says, "And then we'll show you exactly how claimed you are tonight."

A shiver of excitement runs through me as I sit, watching them go to the bar, making me a plate and pouring my coffee. Damn, my life has taken a complete turn. I never imagined being this happy. I look around the table and see both Gia and Bo staring at me with broad smiles, and I can't help but return it. Our little group of misfits is finding their happiness. I meet Bo's eyes and mouth, "You're next."

His eyes widen, and his hand goes to his chest in mock shock. He's being his usual, playful self, as always, with Gia and me, but I see the sadness in his eyes. He thinks because he's bisexual, he won't find what we have. But I know differently. Bo is amazing and will find the perfect partner or partners. Or maybe Gia is right; he needs both of them to make a Bo sandwich. I grin mischievously and bring my hands up, pressing them together in front of me, imitating a sandwich, and he chuckles, shaking his head.

Kane and Cowboy sit my breakfast in front of me, kissing my head. "Be back in a couple of hours," Cowboy says, standing straight and adjusting his hat. I nod, turning to Kane.

"No going anywhere alone," Kane says, giving me a pointed look, and I grin. They then turn and leave the room, and I watch their sexy, firm asses in those tight jeans as they walk out.

I see movement at the main door; Sammy and Nonno enter the clubhouse. They say a brief hello to my men, then come straight to the dining room to find

Gia, followed by their men. They all take seats and begin scanning the room. I wish them a good morning and start eating.

I listen to the conversation around the table as I eat. Blaze and Gia fill Sammy and Nonno in on yesterday's events. Their expressions go stone cold, and their postures become rigid. My gaze shifts, watching the men who came with them. They've paused, taking in the conversation. "We'll handle the mayor," Sammy says in a low, deadly tone, leaning back in his chair.

Blaze nods, and Gia grins. "We'll handle the Diablo's," Blaze says with finality before looking around the room. "Spread the word. Emergency church in 3 hours, all prospects on patrol except 3," he says, and his eyes meet mine. "Three prospects will be with you when Kane and Cowboy can't." His words are final, and I nod. Shit, after yesterday knowing that Gia and I are targets, I'm not complaining.

My eyes go to her, and her expression is a mix of emotions. "I'm staying with Blaze until this is over. We'll talk later," she says, tossing me a wink. I return the wink, but something tells me there's more she's not saying in front of everyone. I guess I'll find out later, I think as I drink the last of my coffee and stand to take my dishes into the kitchen.

I halt my steps when Blaze calls out again. "Mia, you need to attend the meeting."

I turn, looking at him with raised brows. Then it hits me: Kane and Cowboy are claiming me in church. Being theirs means I'll have a seat at the table during meetings. I grin and nod before taking my dishes into the kitchen. Life keeps changing for me.

I called Sal to get updates on the gym and warehouse and to discuss the apartment complex and the clinic. He picks up on the third ring. "Hey, Mia." I hear a loud noise in the background, making it hard to understand him.

"I'm just checking in for an update. We need to discuss the next two projects. Can you meet me in the morning at the apartment complex?" I ask, biting my bottom lip, hopeful. I really want to stay at the clubhouse today.

"Things are moving along here, but we ran into an issue," he says as I hear him moving further away from the noise and a door opening and closing. "The men's locker room had a leak. We had to remove some sheetrock to find it. With replacing the pipes and sheetrock and getting rid of the mold, our timeline is looking to be three weeks."

I sigh. "OK, I understand and will let Gia know. How about meeting me tomorrow morning at the apartments?"

"Sure, how does 9 am sound?" Sal asks, and I nod before remembering he can't see me.

"That works great. See you then." I hit the end call button. Walking upstairs to make the bed and straighten our room. I make a mental note to tell Gia the timeline for the gym.

Chapter 14

Kane

With a roar, Cowboy and I park in the parking lot of the clinic. I shut off my bike and take a minute to stare up at the building while Cowboy gets his hat. I know damn well I'm clean, but Mia needs to know for sure. Fuck, I don't blame her. I could kick myself in the ass for all the meaningless fucks I've had over the years. Trying like hell to chase away painful memories or relieve stress. None of it was worth it.

I'm not sure how I would feel if Mia made the same mistakes I had. Wondering who she had been with would eat me up inside. I reach up, rubbing my chest as it clenches at the thought. If I could take it all back, I would. It wouldn't make me want her any less, but the not knowing versus the pain of knowing would probably kill me. I'm a possessive son of a bitch.

"Let's get to it," Cowboy says, stomping towards the clinic, and I throw my leg over my bike, following him inside. The receptionist gives us both a disapproving look when we tell her we're there for test results, but I ignore it. As soon as we're seated, we get called back. A nurse takes us into a side room, handing each of us our papers. I guess they want us out of here as soon as possible. I take mine, fold it, and walk right back out. Everyone will receive better treatment at the Freedom Clinic.

With wearing a cut, most pass judgment quickly, but getting results for STDs makes it worse. Medical professionals should conduct themselves better. Even receptionists. I toss her my don't fuck with me look as I pass, walking out, and she visibly cringes, stepping back. Good, maybe a little scare will teach her a lesson for the next person who comes in for results.

I stop next to my bike and open the report. Knowing and seeing are two different things, I guess. With a smirk, I read down the list, all negative. I fold it up and tuck it into my back pocket. I see Cowboy doing the same with a grin. "We're good to go," I say, throwing my leg over the bike and pulling the key from my pocket.

Cowboy gives me a chin lift while sitting on his bike, but doesn't make a move to start it. He rests his forearms on the handlebars and stares at me. "We need to talk about who's taking her first." He removes his cowboy hat and runs his hand through his hair.

I want to be her first, and he sees it. We stare at each other for a long time. Cowboy is the one who breaks the silence. "Fuck, I want to be inside her as bad as you. But I'm not sure I'll be gentle enough. I can be..."

I interrupt him, knowing what he's going to say next. "Ya, I've heard things." I don't want to hear shit he's done with other women. All I care about is Mia.

Cowboy nods, and his jaw flexes. "I'll get her ready, and you take her first."

Images of Mia beneath me, writhing while I enter her for the first time, flash in my head and I have to push them away. My growing cock and tingling balls will make for an uncomfortable ride back to her. "Good," I say, but I can't hide the smile forming. "One more thing." I give Cowboy a pointed look. "I've seen your toy chest in the closet. No way you're using shit on Mia, that's touched another woman. So get rid of it."

"Fine, I'll buy new," Cowboy says, putting his hat inside the saddlebag and strapping his helmet on. "Let's stop by the adult store on Buckston Avenue before we head back."

It isn't long before we're pulling into the parking lot of 'Playtime.' I shut my bike off and lower the kickstand, quickly scanning the area out of habit. Nothing seems off, so I dismount and remove my helmet, looking at the displays in the windows. This place might not be so bad. Sexy lingerie on mannequins, games and fuzzy handcuffs seems innocent enough.

I enter with Cowboy, and a woman behind the counter raises her head and grins when she sees him. "How can I help you, gentlemen?" she asks, smiling between us. I nod but say nothing.

"I'll help myself," Cowboy says, going straight for the back of the store, where we pass by several aisles of dildos. Damn, some of these are huge. Do women really use these things?

My eyes sweep further up the shelves, and I stop on a box with an ass and pussy visible inside. I step closer, picking it up for closer inspection. It's silicone and fake as hell. Do men look at this and feel the urge to stick their cock in it? I just want to throw it against the wall and see if it sticks. Nothing could compare to the real thing.

I toss it back on the shelf. I'm ready to leave. When I find Cowboy, he is going from one area to another, grabbing things. Fuck, he knows where everything is like he stocked the damn place.

My eyes widen, and I see all he has in his arms as I approach him: handcuffs, a vibrator, leather cuffs with straps, butt plugs, a ball gag. I reach out, grasping his shoulder. "Brother, do we need all of that?" I ask, and he gives me the 'Are you stupid look.'

"Yes, now grab a bullet from over there," he says, nodding to my left. After a minute of scanning the area he was talking about, I found them. I take one, walk to the front of the store where he's being rung up, and lay it on the counter.

"Looks like a fun night for you two," the lady comments, and my eyes widen.

Oh, hell no. She thinks we're a couple. "We're not using this shit on each other," I say. Cowboy's laughing so hard he's doubled over, hanging onto the counter. That shit isn't funny, and I toss him a nasty look.

"We don't judge here," the lady chirps happily, giving me a mischievous smile.

"Neither do I, but we.." I shake my head, pointing between Cowboy and me, "Are not a thing."

"Ok," she says with a smirk, and fucking Cowboy is howling with laughter. Fuck them for enjoying my embarrassment; I think as I spin on my heel, walking outside. I have nothing against same-sex couples, but I was uncomfortable already in there. Her thinking that I would use that shit on my brother just made it worse.

Grabbing my helmet, I put it on, straddling my bike and scanning the area while I cool down. Cowboy is chuckling as he exits the store, tossing me a wink, and stuffs the bags into the saddlebags. I start my engine and rev it to annoy him.

In 30 minutes, we're at the clubhouse. I need to see my woman. When I reach the main room, I slide my phone from my pocket to call her just as Cowboy steps to my side. Hunter's words stop me. "She's in her office."

I give him a chin lift in thanks and take off in that direction with determined steps. The door is open when I reach it, so I don't stop. My beautiful Mia is sitting at her desk typing away on the laptop. When she raises her head and sees me, her eyes light up. Fuck, this woman is everything.

I walk around, pulling her out of the chair to my chest. "Missed you," I say before taking her luscious lips with mine, pushing my tongue in to taste her mouth. I take my time with the kiss as my hands roam her back down to her full hips. When we pull away, her eyes flutter open, and she looks dazed. I love the effect I have on her.

I reluctantly release her, knowing Cowboy wants to say hello; it's only moments before he has her in his arms. He devours her mouth like he hadn't eaten in weeks. Holy hell, that's hot. I reach down, adjusting myself as I watch her threading her hands into his hair, almost knocking his hat off.

I reach into my pocket, pulling the test results out, unable to wait another minute for her to know we'll be claiming all of her. Not just in church, but physically. Hell, anyway, we can.

Mia looks at my hand and then takes it, looking up into my face. I nod for her to go ahead. She unfolds it, and her eyes roam down the list with a grin. She looks up at me with a grateful expression. "Thank you."

"There's no need to thank me, dreamcatcher," I say, stroking her cheek. Cowboy hands her his, and she does the same, thanking him.

He cups her face with both hands; his loving expression matches how I feel. "Never thank us for doing anything that takes care of you. That's our job as your men," he says, kissing her forehead.

"Church now," Blaze booms, walking down the hallway towards his office with Gia.

I take Mia's hand as excitement goes through me. I've been waiting for this moment. I glance at Cowboy, who gives me a knowing look as we all make our way into church, taking our seats. As soon as my ass hits my seat, I pull Mia onto my lap, wrapping my arms around her. Ya, she has a chair, but I need her close.

Cowboy gives me a scowl that I beat him to it, and I grin. He sits, gripping Mia's thigh firmly, and we watch our brothers enter and get settled.

Chapter 15

Cowboy

I rest my hand on Mia's thigh and get comfortable as my brothers take their seats in church. Blaze has a blank expression but a gleam in his eye that I haven't seen before. I shake my head and ignore it.

Blaze slams the gavel down, calling the meeting to order. "Before we start, I have a few things to address," he announces, scanning the room. "For obvious reasons, Gia, and Mia aren't to leave the clubhouse without an escort." Then he glances at Gia, who nods at him with a smile.

"We also have an announcement," Blaze smirks, pulling Gia's chair closer. His expression shows pride as he looks back at us.

"We found out this morning we're expecting," Gia says, and I see it now. She's glowing, and her smile's radiant.

I've never seen Blaze happier, and I congratulate them both. Then I instinctively tighten my hold on Mia's thigh. Visions of her round with our child growing in her belly have my pulse picking up and my dick twitching. Soon, I tell myself as my eyes roam her body to her beautiful face.

She focuses on Gia with excitement. Her happiness for them is clear. I see Mia turn her head in Bo's direction, and they exchange a look I can only describe as understanding passing between them. He nods to her. The dynamics of their trio are shifting. I need to include Bo more.

He and Hawk are busy with the underground, but I wonder if he would be interested in prospecting. He's already one of us. I'll talk to him later over a beer.

"Now, new business," Blaze says, interrupting the chatter. "Hawk, Bo, is everything set for tomorrow's fight night?" he asks, looking at them. I listen as they talk for a minute, and things move along. I want to jump to where we claim our woman, and Kane's fidgeting tells me he feels the same.

"We're hitting the Diablo's Clubhouse tonight. Axel put half the prospects on patrol while we're gone, the other half at the clubhouse on high alert. We'll arm up and head out at 10 pm." Axel nods, and the rest voice our enthusiasm by beating our fists on the table. Hell, yes, it's about time we took those sons of bitches out.

Blaze turns to Kane and me with a raised brow. "Any other new business?" Fuck yes, there is, and he knows it.

I sit straight and take Mia's hand in mine. "Mia's our old lady. Anybody got a problem with that?" I ask, looking around the table, hearing chuckles and my brothers thump the table with their approval.

Kane wraps his arms around her, pinning hers to her side, making her laugh. "She's been claimed I just had to wait for her to agree. Your cut's ordered, and we'll get you inked soon, dreamcatcher." As soon as the words leave his mouth, Mia stiffens, and her eyes go wide. Humm, she forgot that part.

Her eyes lock on mine, and her lips part. "Can I decide where and what it is?"

I chuckle, leaning in and kissing her cheek. "We'll discuss it later, baby," I say, and she nods, relaxing back into Kane. When we formed the club, we all agreed that if we ever took an old lady, they would wear our ink. No stipulations were made as to what or where. But we're all possessive sons of bitches and knew we'd want to mark what was ours. For Blaze and Gia, it was matching bands tattooed on their fingers. We'll figure out what works for us. I side-eye Kane, and he gives me a chin lift, telling me he's on the same page.

Blaze ends the meeting once we iron out the details of taking down the Diablo's and discuss how to handle any women we find. I immediately stand, pulling Mia with me. As soon as she's on her feet, I toss her over my shoulder and march out while Kane is hot on my heels, chuckling.

I'm not waiting another minute to claim her, and neither is he.

Blaze calls out after us, laughing, "Take it easy on her, brothers."

"She may need a few days off," Kane retorts over the laughter.

Our boots echo in the hall as we head towards the stairs. My woman squeals and squirms; her laughter is delicious, and I can't help but slap her ass, loving the way it reverberates against my palm. Kane's stride matches mine, his eyes glued to Mia's bouncing backside. He grunts his approval, a low rumble that vibrates in his chest. I know what's going through his mind because it's crawling through mine, too—anticipation so rich and heady I can taste it.

We reach our room, and I kick the door open with a swift kick of my boot. The slap of wood against the wall gives way to silence, except for Mia's giggles. Kane closes the door behind us with an audible click, locking out the rest of the world.

"I'm not some sack of potatoes, Cowboy," Mia protests as I lower her onto the bed.

"No, dreamcatcher, you're better than any sack of potatoes," Kane says as he shrugs off his cut, laying it onto the nearby chair. His shirt follows shortly after, revealing flexing muscles, and Mia's eyes are glued to him.

His words ignite a fire in Mia, and she wets her plump lips in anticipation. I unbuckle my belt, my thick fingers working over the worn leather. She jerks her head in my direction, and her breath hitches when I toss it alongside Kane's discarded clothing. But it's not until my cut joins the growing pile in the chair that her eyes widen with pure lust.

In two steps, I have her standing. As soon as Mia's feet hit the ground, Kane and I corner her against the wall, our bodies closing around her. While I pin her wrists above her head, he dips his face to her neck, inhaling her sweet scent.

As if drawn by an invisible force, my lips seek hers. The taste of her unleashes a torrent of desire within us both.

She gasps for breath between kisses as I dive deep while Kane is attacking her neck. Mia is writhing in our hold and bucking her hips forward, begging for contact where she needs it most.

While Kane holds her pinned to the wall, I kneel in front of her. My fingers find their way to her jeans. I quickly undo them, taking them off and raising my hands to trace the edge of her panties before ripping them off with a feral growl. Her breath hitches as I spread her legs wide open.

She tilts her head back with a moan as I explore her wetness with firm strokes of my tongue. Her body shudders at my touch while Kane lifts his head from her neck to connect his lips with hers. The kiss is harsh and demanding, filled with a raw need that matches the rhythm of my tongue, delving into her sweetness.

Her moans grow louder as she grinds herself against my face, desperate for more contact. I feast on her relishing every whimper and gasp that she makes.

Kane works at relieving her of the remaining fabric barrier between them.

Mia squirms against us, her thighs squeezing my head as an orgasm hits her. I drink it all in before slowly standing, my lips glistening with her arousal.

She breaks away from him with a gasp. He looks at me, and I nod, stepping back.

Kane picks Mia up behind her thighs, and she instinctively wraps her arms and legs around him. He carries her to the bed, placing her in the center. He braces himself on his elbows, and strokes her hair with a hand, staring into her eyes. "I've dreamt of this moment, dreamcatcher." Kane rocks his hips, running his dick through her folds. Mia's eyes go wide when he nudges against her entrance.

"Kane," she whispers, as if it's a plea. I lay on the bed next to them, stroking her hair with one hand while I fist my dick with the other.

I watch the expression on Mia's face as he enters her with one powerful thrust. Her eyes clamp shut, and she lets out a moan that sends shivers down my spine as she adjusts to being filled. His hands cradle her face as he holds her perfectly still until she opens her eyes.

"Move," she moans, clutching his shoulders tight. Fuck, I'm aching as I watch Kane pull his hips back and start a slow pace. "Oh," she wails, and Kane's face contorts.

"Fuck, Mia, you're squeezing me so tight I can't hold back." Kane slams into her, and Mia screams out into the room. Damn, her orgasms were so close together.

I squeeze my cock to hold back my own so I don't nut before I'm even inside her. They cling to each other as their bodies jerk and twitch. Kane takes her mouth in a sweet kiss before he slides out of her. I immediately roll her onto my chest, stroking her hair and back. "Are you okay, baby?"

Mia raises her head, giving me a sweet smile. Her face is flushed, and her eyes look dazed. "I'm better than ok," she says, raising her body and rubbing against me. Fuck, she feels so good; my hips jerk up on their own.

I cup her face and kiss those full, luscious lips. I nibble and tease until Mia spreads her legs wide and begins rubbing her dripping pussy against me.

Not able to take it anymore, I pull back from the kiss, reaching one hand between us. She sits up straight and I fist my cock, lining it up. She's wild and ready for more.

"Ride me, baby," I growl, guiding her down onto my pulsing length. A breathy moan escapes her lips as I fill her, bottoming out against her womb. "Cowboy," she cries with almost a shocked expression, and I grind into her, making sure my pelvis rubs her clit as I push even deeper. Mia's mouth drops open, and we both groan out at the pleasure.

She rocks her hips, sliding up and down with a slow, torturous rhythm. My hands grip her waist, guiding her movements as I thrust up to meet her. The sight of her straddling me, and riding my cock is a vision straight out of my fantasies.

Her head rolls back as she rides me faster, her breasts bouncing with every powerful slam of our bodies. Kane watches from the edge of the bed, his hand working over his slick cock as he takes in the erotic display.

The feel of Mia's slick walls contracting around me sends waves of pleasure coursing through my veins. I watch her body move above me, every rise and fall sending shockwaves of pure ecstasy along my spine. Her soft moans turn into ragged cries as she chases another peak.

Kane comes around behind her, his fingers tracing the curve of her back before circling around to play with the sensitive nub between her thighs. When he reaches the other hand down to her ass, playing with her rosebud, she shrieks at the added stimulation and rides me harder.

"Mia," I growl when I feel my climax approaching fast. Every thrust propels us closer to oblivion together.

Kane's hand leaves Mia's clit, and he shifts behind her. I can tell he's stroking his cock to the rhythm she's riding me as he fingers her ass. His heavy breathing becomes more erratic, signaling his impending release.

Suddenly, Mia clamps down on me like a vice as she screams our names. I grit my teeth and watch her beautiful face as her orgasm overtakes her.

My gaze goes down to where our bodies meet. They're glued to where she meets my girth with every bounce and shift of her hips. The sight is so erotic my balls draw tight, and I erupt with a roar.

Holding her hips in place, I throb and pulse, jerking with my release. I swear I feel my soul leave my body and see stars behind my eyes.

Vaguely, I hear Kane growling, and then the weight of both of their bodies drops onto mine. Damn, I couldn't move if I wanted to. I embrace them as we lay in a tangled mess, trying to catch our breaths.

Chapter 16

Mia

A rollercoaster of emotions overwhelms me as I stand here clutching Gia's hand. The steady flow of motorcycles rumbles out of the parking lot, followed by a box truck driven by one of Sammy's men. All of them, armed, headed for the Diablo's clubhouse. This day has gone from the best day of my life to worrying they will be injured or worse.

Bo comes over and throws his arms around our shoulders. "I swore I'd look after you two, and keeping you from worrying is part of it. Let's go inside," he says, leading us into the clubhouse.

"I need a snack to calm my stomach," Gia says, and we follow her to the kitchen. We're all quiet as we gather crackers, cheese, peanut butter and grapes, taking them into the dining room. A couple of prospects join us as we quietly eat. It's like the silence is deafening.

I can't take it anymore, and I glance at Gia. "I'm so happy that you're pregnant."

Gia smiles, then scrunches her nose. Blaze has become more overbearing now. "I pushed him out of the bathroom earlier so I could pee in private," she says, shaking her head.

I giggled at that, and I felt some of the tension ease. Picking up a grape, I remember my conversation with Sal. "There's a delay with the gym. They found a water leak that caused damage and mold. So, it will take about a month to complete," I tell her, and the disappointment is clear. "I'm going to get a crew moving on some apartments and the garage," I continue, and she nods.

"Mia, since you're so good at problem-solving," a prospect says, drawing my attention to the table next to us. I turn and face him. "There's an issue at the bar, and nobody can agree on a fix."

"What's the problem?" I ask, raising my eyebrows. I haven't heard of any issues at Angel's.

"Business is dead—the same handful of girls from the city every week and the same guys. Thor needs new customers," he says, and the prospect nearest him mumbles something about definitely more women under his breath.

I shake my head, knowing what the problem is. "Tell me if I'm wrong here," I say, meeting each of their eyes. "Are these the women you all boast about sharing for a release?" They nod but look confused, and I glance at Gia with a 'Are they stupid' expression. She grins but says nothing as she continues eating. I bite the inside of my cheek to keep from calling them out on their lack of common sense.

I turn fully, facing them, and take a deep breath. "Let me try to explain this. They are your club girls. They may not live or come to the clubhouse, but that's just geography. Bunnies, candy, club girls, whatever you want to call them. That's what they are," I say, pointing to them, and recognition shows in their expressions.

"Now let me get this straight. You want women to come to a bar that's full of club girls? Who screw you guys in the hallway and bathrooms? Hell, I've even heard a story of doing it right on a pool table." Their smiles fade as what I'm saying sinks in. Most women want nothing to do with what I'm describing.

"Clean the place up if you want new customers," I say, then turn around. My words seem to have confused them more, and I roll my eyes at Gia.

She swallows her food and looks at them. "Just tell Thor to come talk to Mia. She'll give him ideas to help." They nod at her, and I dip my head down to hide my smile. Why are guys so clueless sometimes? A deep rumble comes from beside me, and I peer at Bo. His whole body vibrates with laughter, and he shakes his head.

"When was your last visit to Angel's?" I ask with a raised brow in challenge.

He matches my challenging look with one of his own. "You know, when the last time was. Contrary to what you might believe, not all men nail everything that moves," he says with a grin.

He's right; Bo is one of the good ones. I lean over, resting my head on his shoulder, and sigh. "I want you to have the same happiness as Gia and I."

Bo kisses the top of my head and leans closer. "One day, maybe."

It's three long hours before we hear bikes roaring into the parking lot. We all get to our feet and rush outside. I need to check on Kane and Cowboy.

When I reach the parking lot, my heart skips a beat when I see them parking. Rushing forward, I halt just steps away when I can make them out clearer in the darkness. Dried blood is splattered on Kane's shirt and neck, and Cowboy has fresh blood running down his arm to his hand.

Unable to contain myself, I move forward to inspect them closer as they dismount. They both crush me in an embrace that has all the air leaving my lungs. "We're ok," Kane says. The scent of leather fills my nostrils as I breathe deep. It's welcoming.

"Speak for yourself," Cowboy retorts, and I push on his chest to move back so I can see.

"You've been shot," I gasp, covering my mouth.

"Let's get inside so I can clean it. He may need a stitch or two," Kane says, taking my hand. I grasp Cowboy's, pulling him with us. I need to touch them to know they're really okay.

I glance around as we enter the main room. Some crowd around the bar to celebrate, while others go to the tables, waiting for Kane to examine them.

I lead Cowboy to a vacant seat and push him into it, making him chuckle. I begin removing his cut and shirt. Of all the days to wear one, it's the day I need it off to see his injury. He places his large hand over my shaky ones, and I stare into his warm brown eyes.

"I'm ok, baby. The bullet just grazed me. Slow down and take a breath," he says, and I let his words calm me.

"Ok," I breathe out and begin lifting his shirt. He raises his arms, and I pull it over his head. My eyes immediately go to his bloody shoulder. It's a straight line cut through his flesh about a half-inch wide and two inches long. It's deep, though, which explains all the blood. I take his shirt, folding it up to apply pressure while Kane goes to get his medical bag.

"Breathe," Cowboy says again, and I manage a half smile, breathing in through my nose and out through my mouth before nodding. He's here and okay. They're both okay. Cowboy places his hand on my lower back, and the warmth radiating from it is comforting. I melt into his touch when he rubs small circles with his thumb.

I glance around at the other Outcasts while we wait for Kane to return. Thankfully, none of them were seriously injured. I lean forward and kiss Cowboy's head like he does mine when I need contact. "Tell me everything."

Kane returns just as Cowboy goes through the highlights, and I sit so he can attend to his wound. I listen to what happened in shock before relief that it's over settles in. The Diablo's are no more. They got them all, including the president. Five women were being held waiting to be auctioned, and they're being transported to Wells City for treatment, courtesy of Sammy and the D'Angelo's.

After Kane finishes with Cowboy's wound, I follow him around to each man, helping him clean them up and watching as he stitches those who need it. Seeing him work, I realize just how skilled he is. I wonder what his plans are for the clinic. I want to hear everything he and Cowboy plan on doing in the future.

Once we're finished, I realize how tired I am as we climb the stairs together. I walk ahead of them, starting the shower while they undress. They took such good care of me today after claiming me with a bubble bath and whispering sweet words. Now, I need to take care of them. I step back and undress while my eyes roam their bodies. My love for these two men is beyond what I thought possible for another person.

Once we're naked, I open the large shower door and take both of their hands, stepping in.

The steam rises around us, creating a haze in the bathroom. I help wet their tired bodies, aching from tonight's events. Sensing their exhaustion, I reach for the soap and washcloth.

Taking my time, I run the cloth over Cowboy's powerful arms. His muscles flex under my touch. Despite his wound, his eyes lock onto mine, full of heat and desire. My heart skips a beat as he moves closer, but I push him back.

"Not now," I whisper, pressing a light kiss to his lips. "Let me take care of you."

Keeping my gaze on his, I slide the soapy cloth down his broad chest, carefully tracing every line and curve. There's an intensity in his eyes that mirrors my feelings. Its raw need mingled with tenderness.

Next is Kane; I grab a clean washcloth and lather it. The sight of his naked body sends a shiver down my spine despite the steamy heat surrounding us. His hand cradles the back of my neck as I scrub him down. He leans into my touch, letting out a sigh of relief as if this simple act of caring is all he needs.

I watch as they both relax, their gruff exteriors turning soft under my hands. The fear and uncertainty from earlier finally leaves me.

After rinsing them off, we step out of the shower. I grab towels for each of us and dry them off, paying extra attention to Cowboy's wound to ensure it stays clean. With each stroke, I fall a little more in love, his groans only adding to the intensity of my feelings.

While Kane massages my shoulders, I can feel his body pushing into mine from behind. His touch is electrifying, making my body vibrate with anticipation. He leans in, placing soft kisses along the nape of my neck. He knows how to drive me crazy.

With a husky voice that sends shivers down my spine, he murmurs against my skin, "Relax." My knees buckle slightly at his tender touch, and he wraps his arms around me to steady me.

Meanwhile, I continue drying Cowboy, moving lower to his well-defined abs and further down until I reach his semi-hard length. My touch seems to ignite something in him, and before I know it, he's hard, a low growl vibrates from his chest.

"You're such a tease," he breathes as I circle my fingers around him, working his entire length.

Kane's hands travel from my shoulders down to my breasts, kneading them while pressing soft kisses over my shoulder blade. The sensation of their touch is overwhelming, but in the best way possible.

I pick up my pace, stroking Cowboy and his hips jerk forward, meeting my strokes. "Fuck, Mia," he groans out, grabbing the vanity for support with one hand, the other, he threads into my wet hair.

The overwhelming need to taste him hits me, and I look up into his eyes. "Teach me to please you," I say as I lower to my knees. Kane bends with me, never releasing my breasts.

Cowboy's gaze darkens with hunger as he watches me kneel, and his grip on my hair tightens. He guides me, his hands firm yet gentle. "Open your mouth," he orders, the rough timbre of his voice sending a thrill down my spine.

Kane's fingers continue to knead my breasts, increasing my need and desire. I feel him shift behind me; then he pulls me back positioning me. Then I feel his hardness press at my opening, and I shiver with anticipation as he grips my hips tight.

Taking Cowboy deeper into my mouth, I press my tongue to the underside of his shaft as he reaches the back of my throat. "Yes, like that," he groans, encouraging me to go further.

Kane removes a hand from my hip, sliding it around over my stomach to delve between my thighs. His fingers trace over my clit, teasing and coaxing moans from me that vibrate around Cowboy and earn a growl in response.

I feel a flood of sensations as Kane's skilled hands stroke me, tasting and feeling Cowboy on my tongue and lips. Our loud groans of pleasure fill the room.

With each passing moment, their movements become more insistent. Kane thrusts his massive dick inside of me, making me gasp around Cowboy. The stretch and burn sends jolts of pleasure throughout my body. I brace my hands on Cowboy's thighs as Kane begins a relentless rhythm pounding into me.

Cowboy's grip on my hair tightens as he growls and begins fucking my mouth. The raw, primal need rolling off them is coursing into me.

My body shakes in response to Kane's powerful thrusts and him rubbing my clit.

I feel myself spiraling out of control, I'm at their mercy.

I move a hand from Cowboy's thigh, I'm determined to take him with me. I cup his balls and begin massaging them as I take him deeper and fasten my lips around him, setting a pace in tandem with Kane's thrusts.

The tight coil in my stomach unravels, and I moan around Cowboy as the orgasm crashes over me with such force my body shakes. My walls clench around Kane's cock, and he groans out, burying himself deep as he pulses inside of me.

Everything becomes a blur except for their hands gripping my body and ragged breaths that echo in the steamy bathroom.

"Swallow," Cowboy orders in a raspy voice above me. I swallow several times as he releases jets of come into my mouth. His body jerks as curses leave his lips, and his hold on my hair tightens.

Kane's arms come around me in a warm embrace as I pull away from Cowboy. "Holy shit," Cowboy says, falling back against the vanity for support.

Chapter 17

Kane

I'm finishing the last of my bacon and eggs, tuning out the surrounding conversations until Thor sits across from Cowboy Mia and me. His chair creaks as he scoots it up to the table and stares at Mia. I watch her sit her fork down and raise an eyebrow, waiting for him to speak.

Thor clears his throat and rests his elbows on the table. "I heard you have some ideas to bring business to the bar."

I side-eye Cowboy to see if he's watching this, too, and his lip twitches in amusement. Mia has told us her thoughts, and Thor won't like them all.

"I've been in a few and have some ideas," she says, sipping her coffee. "If you want, Angel's profitable and not just a club bar. You need to do three things."

Thor leans forward with interest, waiting for her to continue. "First, clean it up. This means fresh paint and replacing any worn or broken tables and chairs. Next, get rid of the club girls, or you'll never get other women as patrons." Mia pauses as if in deep thought. "You need food, a deep fryer, and flat top grill for finger foods. You could do a simple menu. Which means hiring a good cook in the kitchen. Last, you need an attractive bartender who is unavailable."

Thor's eyebrows scrunch together. "What do you mean unavailable?"

Mia's smile widens. "The best bars or clubs have attractive bartenders that are friendly but unattainable. A bartender who is good at their job, listens to customers' problems and always has a smile, but turns down advances keeps customers coming back," she says.

"How the fuck am I supposed to make sure they do that? I can't control who people date or fuck," he says, leaning back in his chair. It's not what he said that pisses me off. It's his tone with Mia. I sit straight just as a growl erupts from me.

Thor's eyes lock on me, and he raises his hands in surrender. "I didn't mean anything, man; I'm just frustrated." I nod and try to relax.

Mia grins and places one hand on my thigh and the other on Cowboy, whose body language says he's ready to knock Thor's head off for raising his voice to Mia. He'll have to beat me to it if he does it again.

Mia looks back at Thor and shrugs before answering his question. "Make it part of the hiring process that customers are off-limits."

Thor nods and seems to think over her words. "I like your ideas. I'll have to run everything by Blaze." He thanks her and leaves. When I look at Mia, she shakes her head, watching him walk out.

"What's going through that beautiful head of yours?" I ask, reaching up and stroking her long hair.

"I think they'll do the kitchen and clean the place up but keep the girls. If that happens, Angel's will look nice and have food, but the customers they want won't come," she says, and I nod in understanding.

Cowboy leans closer, kissing her forehead. "You're right, but they'll learn, eventually. I need to handle some club business with Blaze today," he says, eyeing me. I nod so he knows I'll take care of Mia today. He plants a lingering kiss on Mia's full lips before leaving.

Once we clean up our dishes, Mia and I make our way to meet Sal at the apartment complex. The sun has already made the temperature outside almost unbearable, and it's still morning. Thankfully, the wind whipping around us on the ride there kept us cool. Mia and I park our bikes, seeing Sal waiting for us. We do a complete walkthrough of the complex discussing repairs, timelines, and agreeing that he will do one level at a time. He'll bring a small crew in to get started on the first level of the building, so we can rent apartments while they continue renovating the upper levels.

Our next stop is the clinic where Sal meets us. We go through the same process with what I'll need done so I can order supplies and equipment. By the time we return to the clubhouse, it's after 5 pm.

I lead Mia upstairs so we can get ready for opening night at the Underground. Excitement has been buzzing around the clubhouse for it to open. Hawk and Axel both announced this morning that they were registering to fight. So, I know there will be at least two exciting matches happening.

Mia and I get undressed and enter the shower. I back her under the spray, helping her wet her hair so I can shampoo it. Sometimes, I think I get as much pleasure out of caring for her as she does when I do it.

I'm working her hair into a lather when the door opens, and Cowboy joins us with a grin. He leans down, capturing Mia's mouth with his. "Missed you today, baby," he murmurs. His eyes meet mine over Mia's shoulder, and I see a challenge. I quirk an eyebrow as he grabs her hips, spinning her towards me.

I waste no time grabbing her and meeting her gaze. "Jump," I order, and she does. Her legs wrap around my waist and her arms around my neck.

Cowboy leans in close, pressing his body into her back while he brings his mouth to her ear. "You're going to take us both, aren't you, baby?"

Mia moans at his words and begins rocking her sweet little pussy against my painfully hard cock. Fuck yes is all I can think as I rock with her, letting my shaft run through her wet folds. "Good girl," I say, tightening my hold on her as Cowboy massages her ass behind her while stroking himself.

I shift my hips so I'm lined up at her entrance and push forward. Mia groans, and her eyes go wide as I fill her up. Her walls clench down on me as I bottom out, and she gasps. "You're so big," she says as a jolt of pleasure shoots up my spine at having her wrapped around my shaft so tight. Mia's my heaven.

Her back arches, and she groans out as Cowboy pushes into her tight rosebud. When he rocks his hips slowly, making his way inside, I slide a hand between us. With my thumb, I circle her clit.

Mia's eyes roll back in ecstasy as we take control of her body. I start slow, deliberate thrusts that have Mia cursing and digging her nails into my back.

"Fuck," Cowboy exclaims when he's fully inside her. His eyes meet mine, and his expression looks pained. "So tight, so fucking good," he says, and I feel his words deep in my balls. If I thought Mia was tight before, she is now with us both filling her. As I pull out for another thrust, Cowboy pushes forward. I can feel his every movement through her thin membrane. We're all connected, and the primal need to pound into her is building. I adjust my hold and start a steady rhythm, and Cowboy does the same.

"That's it, baby, take our big dicks," Cowboy says, looking down and watching himself fuck her ass. Mia's eyes open and lock onto mine, and I lose control. She's helpless between us, unable to do anything except be consumed with pleasure. "I'm close," Mia whimpers as her pussy contracts around me.

"Come for us, dreamcatcher," I order and begin a relentless pace, fucking her in earnest. Cowboy's thrusts match mine as we send her soaring with an explosive orgasm.

Fucking hell, I think as she clamps down hard on me. Cowboy curses and throws his head back as Mia screams out into the room with her release. It sends me over the edge with a guttural roar as I slam into her one last time, planting myself deep against her cervix.

Cowboy isn't far behind. A string of curses leave his mouth, and his body jerks. We all cling to each other, pulsating with our release. I drop my head to Mia's shoulder and suck hard, feeling the need to mark her as my vision blurs from the force of that explosive orgasm.

She moans again, letting her head fall back onto cowboy's shoulder while she clings to me. Cowboy latches onto the other side of her neck, and she whimpers. I pull away, and when those beautiful eyes meet mine, I smile before brushing my lips over hers. I put all my love and devotion for her into the kiss. I love this woman more than life itself.

Epilogue

Cowboy

My feet pound against the steps as I make my way up to our room with a smile. The shop finally called saying Mia's cut was ready and I could wait another minute to pick it up. I can't wait to see her wearing it. Once I make it to the landing, Kane comes out of our room, looking from the box to me with a raised brow in question.

"Her cut," I say as I approach him. He grins and reaches for the box. I watch him flip the lid open and pull it out. Kane's eyes have the same spark of possessiveness I felt when the shop showed it to me.

"Tonight," he says, raising his gaze to meet mine.

"Ya, the grand reopening of Angel's is the perfect time with everyone gathering," I say taking the box from him so we can hide it until then. I don't want her to see it before the party. "Where's she at?"

Kane turns, cracking the bedroom door open a few inches, peering inside. "In the closet dressing."

I nod tucking the box under my arm. "You got the rings?" I ask hoping like hell he didn't forget after helping Thor and Hawk decorate for tonight.

Kane grins mischievously and reaches into his pocket, pulling out a ring box. When he flips it open, there are two matching bands. I pull one from the box and examine it. Two silver strands of metal intertwine around a single gold one. It's perfect—a symbol that the three of us are a family with no beginning and no end. I slide it back into the ring box with the other one and nod my approval.

When the door swings open, revealing Mia, we both stand straight, and Kane quickly shoves the jewelry box into his pocket. Mia's smile fades as she glances between us, cocks a brow, and puts her hand on her hip. "What are you two up to?"

I smile, stepping forward and pulling her to me. When her soft, curvy body crashes into mine, I lean down so my mouth is on her ear. "Be patient, baby, and we'll reward you later," I growl. Her body trembles slightly, and she clutches my cut, making me chuckle. Damn, I love how I affect her. My eyes flick over to

Kane, and he looks hungry, so I step back and take her hand. As soon as I do, he has her in an embrace, kissing the hell out of her.

We ride together as a club to Angel's with Blaze and Gia in the front with Axel our enforcer. Normally, it would be our road captain leading, but Axel handles both roles. Next is me as V.P. with Kane and Mia at my side. My club brothers are all at our back. As our engines rumble into the parking lot.

Angel's is lit up with bright lights, a new sign, and fresh paint making it look brand new. I'm impressed with everything they've done. If they were smart and listened to Mia and Gia, they shouldn't have any problems with getting more business now.

I dismount and walk over grabbing my woman from Kane who was helping her off his bike. "You ride back with me baby," I say in a gruff voice. When her legs are wrapped around me I'm in heaven. Whether it's in the bedroom or not. Mia smiles and those beautiful brown eyes sparkle when she locks eyes with me. Damn, I'm a lucky man, I think as I reach down, taking her hand in mine.

We all file in, seeing a prospect behind the bar wiping it down and Hunter drying glasses. Thor marches forward, taking the prospect's place as bartender. Mia pulls us forward with a confused look on her face. "You didn't hire a female bartender?" Her voice was rude or condescending. It came out confused, and all eyes went to Thor.

He sighed resting his hands on the bar as the music from the jukebox grew louder in preparation of the celebration. "Look, I tried. But the only applicants were the regular girls. That defeats the purpose."

Mia nodded, looking in deep thought just as the doors opened again, and I turned along with the rest of the group. We advertised the re-opening in Wells City to draw a crowd. I felt Mia stiffen beside me as a group of women walked in laughing.

The same girls, our regular club girls dressed in just enough to cover their tits and ass come strutting into the bar like they own the place. Big smiles adorned their faces, some twirling loose strands of hair around a finger, but all of them swinging their hips like it was a mating call.

What the hell are they doing here? Just as the thought went through my mind, Mia swirls around on Thor, slamming her hands on the bar. "You didn't listen to what I said at all did you?"

Thor's face turns red, and his eyes are hard at her words. It's a defense mechanism, I know, but he better watch what he says to my woman. I step closer to Mia and raise a brow, daring him to go off on her. Kane takes the same defensive stand on her other side.

Thor raises his eyes to me and takes a breath knowing to cool off before talking to my woman like he would one of us. His face is more relaxed when he shifts his gaze back to Mia. "You were in the club meeting with us. Banning them didn't pass the vote. So here we are, and there they are. I and the other officers won't touch them inside the bar. Any action with them or any other woman has to be off premises."

Mia nods and gets an evil grin. "I understand your predicament. But Thor," she pauses as if for dramatic effect leaning forward. I lean in, too, unwilling to miss what she's about to say. "Mark my words you and the club will regret your vote. Right there," she points over to the group of club girls gathered around the prospects rubbing all over them. "When you and your brothers meet a woman you want as your own, you now have walking talking resumes as to how you screw. Women love that," Mia says then stands straight again.

Thor, on the other hand, goes white, and his eyes widen in realization. I chuckle looking down at my amazing woman. "What do you want to drink?"

Mia smiles up at me sweetly as if moments ago she wasn't being a sarcastic little she-devil. "Beer is fine, Thank you."

I nod and order it for her, but Thor doesn't move. He keeps staring at Mia. "I'll get it," Hunter says, shaking his head as he rolls to the cooler, pulling a long neck out and unscrewing the lid. When he slams it onto the bar top it seems to jerk Thor out of his daze.

Thirty minutes later, the conversations are flowing, pool tables are filled, darts are being played, and all is well. My eyes meet Kane's, and he nods, getting up. When he reaches the jukebox, he pulls the plug from the wall. The music stops, and all eyes turn to him. I take Mia's hand, leading her to the center of the room. Kane meets us with the box that holds her cut, handing it to me.

"You've been ours for a while now, baby, but it's time you wore our names. Not just on your skin but on your back," I say, flipping the lid open and pulling her cut out. Mia gasps, covering her mouth as she looks at it.

She looks from me to Kane with both excitement and joy as she grabs us both in a fierce hug. "I love it."

I open the front of it wide when she pulls back, and she immediately turns, putting her arms through the holes and sliding it on. Damn, her face is glowing, making her even more beautiful. My dick starts to twitch at the sight of seeing our names on her. Property of Kane and Cowboy in large letters for all to see is across the back along with club colors. It's very similar to the tattoos we got three days ago on our shoulders. Except they have each other's names above and below the club colors to signify we are a family.

Cheers and well wishes ring out around the bar as Mia runs her hands down the front of it. Tears brim her eyes, and I step closer, taking her hand. Kane does the same, pulling the jewelry box from his pocket. Mia's eyes go wide, watching our every move.

Kane flips the top open with his thumb, and I take one from the box, holding it so he can go first this time since I did her cut. Mia laughs even though a tear escapes down her cheek. Kane kisses her hand before sliding his ring onto her finger. "You're ours in every way, dreamcatcher, and everyone will know it." He takes her face in both hands before kissing her. When he pulls away, she is out of breath and flushed.

I pull on her hand in mine making her turn towards me. "A part of me always thought I'd never have a woman or family. You changed that, you make me want everything. You are my everything, baby," I say, sliding the ring on her finger and then kissing it. "Now and forever."

Mia reaches up, stroking the sides of my face down to my goatee and pinching the hair, making me wince a little. "You better believe it's forever," she says before getting on her tiptoes and kissing me. I hear laughter around us but I don't give a shit. I pick Mia up by the back of her thighs and she wraps her legs around me as I devour that delectable mouth of hers.

She pulls back moments later, looking at me with a quizzical look, then at Kane. "Where are your rings?" she asks and my body goes stalk still. I feel frozen to the spot. Fuck, we hadn't thought of that. I glance at Kane and he has a look on his face that describes how I feel.

Mia wiggles in my grasp and I sit her down. She straightens her cut and looks pointedly between us. "So," she draws out making a point to look down at her fingernails and my gut instantly has a knot in it. "You want me to wear rings showing I'm taken but don't think you should do the same?" Mia raises her gaze to meet mine. She looks my face over, and then she looks at Kane doing the same. I have to fix this.

I step forward, taking her by the waist, and pull her to me. "Baby, we didn't think. We'll go to the jewelry store tomorrow."

Kane comes up behind her, leaning his head down and kissing her ear. "You're right, dreamcatcher. We weren't thinking. We'll take care of it."

Mia smiles up at us with a gleam in her eye and a wide smile. "Good. I love you both more than words can say."

My chest clenches. I know how she feels. There are no words that describe my love for her. It's like nothing I say is enough.

Also by Mel Pate

Firehouse 77

The Hot Fire Chief: Firehouse 77 Book 2

Outcasts MC

Gia: Outcasts MC Book 1

Kane & Cowboy: Outcasts MC Book 2

Standalone

The Fireman Next Door: Firehouse 77 Book 1

9 798223 041412